AF489958

EXTREMELY FORCED CONTENT:

Explicit Rough Daddy Stories, Submission, BDSM, Gay and More

VOL.6

by Rebecca Sin

I would like to invite you to read another one of
my books that I think you will really enjoy.
The book is called:

"EXPLICIT DADDY'S ADULT:
Filthy Hot Stories In Family VOL.4"

Enjoy!

This is a work of fiction. Names, character, places and incidents are either the product of the author's imagination or are used fictitiously, and any resemblance to actual persons, living or dead, business establishments, events or locales is entirely coincidental.

@ COPYRIGHT 2020
by Rebecca Sin

All rights reserved.

No part of this book may be reproduced or used in any manner without written permission of the copyright owner except for the use of quotation in a book review.

FIRST EDITION 2020

Table of Contents

MALE FORESKIN

Forced Circumcision Story

I was fortunate to be left intact while growing up in the cut happy USA. I   have enjoyed all forms of masturbation with my foreskin even up to the day I was able to retract it fully for the first time. I am a married Hispanic, 5'9" 200, athletic build with a nice 8" thick and shaved uncut cock with a very long abundant foreskin.

Prior to meeting and marrying my wife, I have secretly been involved with other circumcised men mainly through their interest in my foreskin. Most early encounters involved meetings through mail correspondence from ads in a swinger magazine picked up at my local adult book stores. Then it progressed to visiting various gay spas around the L.A. area in which I lived. Today I continued to secretly meet local men and couples through Creg-list after I got married. My wife who also loves my foreskin is not acceptable to my bi-sexuality. She kind of has an idea but I know I must keep it from her in order to fulfill my bi-side and foreskin needs.

A personal ad caught my attention. The headlines read, "Docking" with a photo of a cock buried deep inside another mans foreskin. Curious 40, 8.5" professional circumcised male looking for other uncut guys for explore jack off but I'm mainly interested in docking. It interested me as I have tried docking once a long, long time ago and realized it is something that has resurfaced and becoming popular. I figured what a better way to give back to my less fortunate brothers.

I answered the add with an attached photo of my body showing the muscles I have worked extremely hard for and the long piece of foreskin dangling at the tip of my flaccid but thick cock. He was very interested but as most of the ads placed many can not host but we remained in contact through email or instant messaging. We chatted about several fantasy encounters we would play out once we got together. He was able to squeeze out some circumcision talk and role play fantasies of mine.

An opportunity came up as my family was headed out to visit relatives and I was going to be alone for a week. I planned my week accordingly with correspondences I kept in contact with for days like this. Friday night host a bi-married couple interested in a threesome with an uncircumcised male MW4M. Saturday night host a curious married circumcised male into first time foreskin explore and jack off M4M.

Sunday afternoon visit to a local gay spa and met three guys, two circumcised and one uncut. Tuesday night host two gay couple one cut other uncut MM4M. Thursday night host for DOCKING M4M.

Adam was his name. Tall clean cut American 40, just as he appeared in his pictures we exchanged. I knew he had a foreskin fetish and was very upset at his parents for having him circumcised. He talked a lot about his failed attempts to stretch and restore so he plainly gave up and focused his attention to enjoying the feeling of being inside of other intact foreskins.

He took his time checking out and exploring my cock, balls, shaft then foreskin. During his play he asked if I had ever thought about getting circumcised and I told him that when I was younger. I was just getting sexually active and I became discouraged when meeting women who knew nothing or interested in a guy with foreskin. Rejection after rejection I began to think about getting myself circumcised. Since then the thought of being circumcised did run through my mind from time to time. It made for some good circumcision talk, fantasies while masturbating and role play with the wife. All the exam, foreskin play and circumcision talk got me so hot that he had me dripping pre-cum from the small opening at the tip of my foreskin.

We got together so we can look at our cocks and compare. He was 8.5" long and thick with a big mushroom stood out, flared head, no wrinkles excess skin or anything bunched up behind the glans. His circumcision was invisible. I couldn't tell or see his scar and he had no frenulum at all. Even with his attempts to restore he was still left with a nice and tight circumcision. Mine not so prominent sticking out on my 8" glory compared to his 8.5" cocks but I had a long covering foreskin.

I worked and stretched my foreskin good while I watched him play with his cut cock to full erection. I've had my share of letting cut guys fuck my foreskin and I took control by positioning us head to head. I think he was okay with that as he had little experience. He never had the opportunity to put his cock fully into another man's foreskin. Even though he tried with the other uncut guys but none of them had a long foreskin like I had. I retracted all the way back and put our heads against each other.

Then I worked my foreskin over his big mushroomed head. My foreskin already stretched from the play we both gave it. He then thrust to finish the job by burying his cock deep inside my wet foreskin. He stretched me good as he was a little thicker in the head than I was but my foreskin loved it and had no problem taking him fully.
He got his hand around my foreskin and worked it back and forth paying close attention to his desensitized glans. At the

same time his other hand was groping my buttocks. It was a rhythm to be admired as he focused and worked to stretch my foreskin to cover more of his shaft but the stretching of my foreskin gave me equal sensation. I could tell he was ready to explode by his panting, moaning, thrusting motions and then tightening buttocks. I said don't stop and he immediately knew what to do as he worked himself up to speed. He jacked faster and harder keeping good pressure on the right pressure points. I could feel his head flare inside my worked foreskin and I felt his grip getting tighter as he shot loads and loads into my foreskin. To our amusement we noticed no leak between us. He had a tight seal locked together as his cum shot inside inflating my foreskin full of his cum. I could tell it was an amazing experience for him.

He asked me more about my interest in circumcision and the role play my wife and I had from time to time. I told him my wife gets off when I wear the foreskin retraction device I purchased online. It holds back my foreskin so we can have circumcised sex. All of her boyfriends had been circumcised and I was her first uncut guy so it is hot role play for the both of us. I get to feel what it's like to be circumcised and she gets to pretend she's fucking one of her old boyfriends. I have seen videos and the various tools used and have read some hot letters about detailed circumcisions but other than playing with tools or actually role playing a circumcision I just wear the device. I told him that I love my foreskin very much and would never think about getting myself circumcised. I would have to be forced like in the letters I go back to from time to time where I would not have the opportunity to resist. Once again all this talk about my foreskin and circumcision got my juices flowing.

He said he brought with him a circumcision tool called the Gomco clamp and if I let him he would role play an erotic forced circumcision using the device on me. My heart jumped to the thought of trying something new and I so much wanted to check out the tool personally.

With my approval he went to his car and brought back a suitcase. The Gomco clamp is a metal device with a bell-shaped end. During circumcision using a Gomco clamp, the foreskin is stretched over the bell, and the clamp is tightened over the foreskin. The foreskin is cut away and the clamp is removed.

He had me tied up on the table. He began to run his fingers up and down my body and positioned himself between my legs. Immediately I began to get hard. My manhood hardened and I consider myself to be thick and my foreskin dark brown and abundant which still bunched up at the tip of my erect cock. I have lots of foreskin and an overall nice proportionate looking cock. He reached down and cupped my balls in his hands. He then gently sucked on my nipples. After working my balls and ass, He moved slightly to the base of my cock. He has big hands and my thick cock filled it fully as he wrapped his hands around it. He began to slowly stroke back my foreskin to reveal my cock head. It glistened with precum as it was fully retracted and in view for him to see.

Moist and tender looking, it looked so sensitive and vulnerable to the elements it was about to encounter. The cool air and slight abrasion and tug of the foreskin sliding back and forth as he gently stroked it. The underside revealed my long thin frenulum which allowing for full unrestricted retraction. I began to squirm and moan in pleasure. He held my foreskin back tightly and stretched my frenulum. He placed two fingertips on it and began to knead the underside of my exposed glans. It sent spikes of pleasure through my spine as he manipulated my sensitive frenulum. I threw my head back in ecstasy while shouting out obscene words. He reached for my drooling cock. I was so wet and hard it was unbelievably slick.

He stroked my cock a while before he bunched my foreskin up at the top. He began to insert his finger into my cum soaked foreskin and began to finger my insides. I continued to moan and raised my ass up off the table. My pre cum now dripping down my shiny shaft and down between my ass and soaking the table. He spent some time finger fucking my foreskin with his fingers before he switched to another technique. He grabbed my foreskin and held it between both thumbs and forefingers and began to pull and stretch it up as far as it would go. With so much skin, he was able to create and look down the funnel of foreskin created.

With every tug, I moaned louder and would thrust for more. I liked the abuse he was giving my foreskin. As he stretched it with his four fingers, he gradually inserted five then six. The pleasure out did the pain as he tugged, stretched and finally inserted six fingers into my tight foreskin. He stretched it out good as I continued to moan louder. I could feel and clearly see the outlines of his fingers pushing through the skin from the inside as he tugged and stretched harder.

After the stretching workout on my foreskin, he reached into his suitcase pulling out a huge dildo with some lube. I told him I was more of a top than a bottom but he insisted that it will help in loosening me up and heighten my ejaculation during the role play. My wife had once playfully fucked me with her dildo but it wasn't as huge as the one Adam was about to put into me. Before I could say anything more he began to finger fuck me with his fingers and it did loosen me up. I was begging for him to put that monster into my ass. I felt the tip push against my sphincter and then felt the large head pop violently into my hole. The first penetration I yelled and my eyes widened. He let me rest a bit while he pumped on my cock to deaden the pain. The last 12" slide in with no problem coming to resting deep within my bowels.

Next he pulled out an inflatable rubber ball extremely larger than the circumference of my knob. With the amount of pre cum inside my skin, he was able to insert the ball into my foreskin with little resistance. The ball was soon inflating and continued to stretch my foreskin as it was encased completely within. He left me to lay untouched and I moaned from the continuous stretching affect the ball had on my foreskin. He started to pump that large dildo in and out of my ass as my cock began to go into convulsions and began to shoot load after load of cum. My cum oozed out the sides as my foreskin ballooned while trying it's hardest to retain the ball within. The ball held in position as the convulsions subsided. I lay there tied up and all I wanted to do was grab my foreskin to pump all the cum out from my aching balls. Instead I lay there heavily breathing with no assistance shooting load after load. My cock softened a bit, the dildo still buried deep inside my ass. I was still semi erect and wanting more.

Jokingly, he said this will be the last time I would be able to masturbate and pleasure my foreskin like that. Playing along, I just nodded my head. He then

 reached down and grabbed my semi hard cock and gently retracted my foreskin back. The ball popped out and the cum trapped within gently oozed out and down my exposed shaft. He immediately placed his mouth over my exposed glans and began to suck me dry. He bunched my skin up at the top and made sure he sucked every last bit of cum as he cleaned me up with his mouth. At this time I was rock hard again. He positioned himself between my legs and within hands distance. He continued to suck my cock and pay special attention to my foreskin. He then began to bunch up my foreskin at the tip and gently nibbled and chewed on it while rolling my foreskin between his razor sharp teeth. Nothing but moaning filled the room while he continued to nibble and chew on my foreskin. I felt him poke and swirled his tongue inside my foreskin. Encasing his tongue with it, he began to lick the tip and around my cock head from within. I began to lubricate again and I knew he could taste it. I asked if he could taste my cum and he moaned and nodded yes.

Although I shaved before our meet a light shadow had formed already. He grabbed the razor and shaving cream and told me that before any circumcision, the patient had to be shaved completely. He was totally into the game. As he lathered me up, he grabbed the razor from off the table and began to shave me. I played along and cried out that I changed my mind and didn't want the circumcision after all. I wanted to keep my skin so I could continue to masturbate dock and role play with it. I pleaded as he continued to shave me clean. Once the shaving was complete, he would prepare the "Gomco" the circumcision tool.

He took the clamp from off the table and reached over and grabbed my flaccid cock. He drew back my foreskin and rubbed some numbing agent on it. Then he placed the cold cap that covered the entire exposed head of my cock. He then drew the foreskin back over the cap and bunched it up as much skin as he could get. As excited as I was I was flaccid so he was able to grab a hand full of foreskin, which would be removed in the simple operation. I continued to keep myself busy playing the part and it took my mind off what he was doing to my cock. Finally he put on the finishing touches with the clamp. He lowered the clamping device, which then caught my attention when it snapped loudly into place pinching my foreskin enough to cut off the circulation.

I saw my cock become rock hard with the foreskin remained trapped inside the clamp. I felt the pressure of my huge cock expanding but then my foreskin immediately went numb. It felt real enough to make me continue to plead with him to not circumcise me. He pulled out a scalpel and ran it across my shaft to let me see and feel the authenticity of the steel against my skin. My heart raced when I saw the knife. Here I am, I'm tied up, my foreskin numb and I knew we both agreed it wouldn't go past this scenario. I politely asked him to untie me. With a hard on and grin, he said it was too late to turn back now and that it was going to happen if I liked it or not. I told him I wasn't kidding and to untie me. He refused to do so as he moved the knife up towards the clamp and inserted the scalpel into the groove that circled my clamped off foreskin.

I panicked and started to yell and scream for help. He immediately placed a gag into my mouth. He propped my head up and said "I don't want to hear you but I want you to watch what I'm going to do to your foreskin"! He returned to his position and no matter how much I squirmed and tried to get free, he had a strong grip on my cock with one hand and in the other held a knife.

I couldn't believe my eyes as I watched him run the scalpel through the groove. I flinched as I felt the knife tear through and severe my skin. The scene ran back over and over in my mind in slow motion that seemed like it took hours. I laid my head back and collapsed as the operation came to an end. Thank goodness the clamp had numbed my foreskin enough to where I couldn't feel it. I still couldn't comprehend what just happened. I was hoping it was a bad dream. As I lifted my head to refocus on my foreskin, I watched as he slowly lifted off my severed foreskin from the tool. Immediately I could feel the cool air hitting my exposed glans.

Something tells me he wasn't done yet as he stood there with a full hard on and playing with my foreskin. I watched as he stretched it with his fingers like playing with taffy while holding it up in my face making me watch. His fingers were slick and red from the mixture of blood and semen. I was shocked and horrified all I could do was lay and watch still in disbelief wishing that this day never happened.
He stood snuggled up beside me and threw his huge swollen circumcised cock and balls onto my chest. Then holding onto my severed foreskin he stretched it open using his fingers before placing it over his bare glans. With one

hand gripping the foreskin and with the other hand I watched him slide it back and forth as if it was his own. His swollen head was now pushing through the skin and then disappearing again. He took his time working and enjoying my foreskin stroking with his right then switching to his left hand. He was torturing me as I lay and watch him have his way with my skin.

Morning was slowly peaking through the blinds and he was finally showing signs of coming to an end. With the Gomco still attached to my cock resting between my legs the bleeding had stopped. I still lay there tied up, dildo still in my ass, gagged and flaccid on the table. His muscles in his body tightened and his buttocks clinched. His feet began to slowly lifting him into the air forcing his cock closer and closer to my face. He pumped hard on his cock with my skin and shot loads into the air with some of it hitting my face, landing in my hair and leaving a huge puddle under my chin.

He removed my foreskin from his cock and threw it into the puddle of his cum that was still under my chin. He began to remove the Gomco from my cock, pulled the dildo out my ass and placed everything into his suitcase. He collected his things before untying me and headed out the door. I was exhausted and didn't say a word but I slowly got up after I heard him drive away and inspected my cock for damages. It was bruised and swollen but the head was now permanently exposed. I looked around for my foreskin but it was nowhere to be found. The son of a bitch kept it as a token. Too embarrassed to do anything I collected myself and tried to think of a plan to tell my wife what had happened and why I got myself circumcised.

THE GLORYHOLE
Forced Gay For Gloryhole Story

A few years back, when I still lived in the city, I was dating a girl and we had a very kinky relationship. I was her slutty little bi-sexual boyfriend and we had an open relationship. We had a couple of MMF threesomes with guys she knew, and she always got off really well watching me suck on another man, so being bi, I did that just for her. Eventually she began to peg me while I was blowing these guys.

I went along with it all because I enjoyed a lot of it myself, but she seemed to stop letting me fuck her, and I felt like I was only cumming when jerking myself off while she strap on fucked my booty. I got pretty fed up with her fucking guys and ordering me around, making me take it up the ass or in the mouth. I wanted to have a FFM threesome, but she didn't really seem down for that, saying that we both enjoyed fooling around with other men.

So the next time we went to have sex she told me i'd have to let her strap on fuck me for a bit, which is reluctantly agreed to. She lubed up my ass and lubed up her strap on, she had a larger model than usual.

It was about 7 inches long and fairly thick so it was a bit of a task taking it all in, but I managed. I had refrained from cumming for a few days before because I wanted to really enjoy this session. She inched her way into my ass slowly and eventually I felt her thighs on mine. She thrusted in and out of me for a solid 5 minutes before she stopped and asked if I was ready to fuck.

My dick was leaking like a faucet, precum dripping everywhere. I begin to regret taking a few days off of cumming for this. She rolled me over and begin to slowly crawl down towards my cock. She was kissing my body as she made her way down, and eventually, she wrapped her lips around it. I felt like I was gonna burst right then and there. I tried with every fibre of my being to hold out, but it was too late. I tapped her on the head and before she could pull off I exploded inside of her mouth.

Rather than get off. she stayed put and took the entire load in her mouth. After I was done, she stood up and put her hands on my shoulders, leaning in so her face was right on level with mine.

Her mouth was completely full but she grabbed my face with her hand and forced me to open my mouth. Out of her mouth came a giant load of cum, mixed with her saliva, that landed right in my open mouth.

After all of my semen was in my mouth she squeezed my lips shut and told me to swallow. I didn't want to swallow it at all, but I had no where to go, so I reluctantly gulped down 3 days worth of my own semen. I gagged pretty hard at first, but was eventually able to choke it all down. After that she started to insult me.

"Wow you really liked taking it up the ass this time, didn't you," she said sneeringly. "You wanted to fuck me so bad but you couldn't even last 30 seconds?"

I felt pretty ashamed of cumming so fast and not giving her a good fucking. After blowing a load it takes me a while to get back into the mood, and it was just not gonna happen that night.

I woke up the next day and she said she had an idea to spice up our sex life. She was gonna take me down to the local sex shop to buy some more toys. I didn't really think much of it, so I went along. I showered, put on some clothes and ate breakfast then headed down to the sex shop. When we got there she told me she had a big surprise for me and told me to put on a blindfold.

I put it on and then she said she was gonna put a collar on me to guide me around. Once again, I reluctantly agreed. I got out of the car and she had me following her on the leash. I went inside and followed her some more. She conversed with the shopkeeper a bit, telling him I'd arrived. I had no idea what was gonna happen and I was beginning to feel a bit worried.

I asked her what was going on and she told me to calm down, we walked into what felt like a backroom and she was fiddling around with the leash I was on. I felt a chain leash attach and the rope leash detach and next thing I know, i'm getting pulled down to my knees. I immediately reach for my blindfold when some man much stronger than me grabs my hands and handcuffs them behind my back.

Next thing I know, I'm stuck on my knees, face up against a wall with about 6 inches of give on the chain.

My girlfriend decided to undo my blindfold at this time, and there I was. Face to face with a glory hole, a chain going through another small hole underneath it, forcing me to stay in place.

"Isn't this what you wanted honey," she said with a bit of a laugh. "You told me before that you always wanted to try out a glory hole, well now is your big shot!"

I had confessed to her sometime before that I thought it'd be hot to suck dick at a gloryhole, but that I'd never want to go through with it. I told her to untie me immediately and after a bit of back and fourth, I heard a door open on the other side of the wall. I heard footsteps inching closer and closer to the hole, and suddenly, I heard something unzip. Next thing I know, I'm looking through the hole at some guy's flaccid penis.

"I hope you're hungry," he said as he began to rub it. "I haven't cum in a while and I got a big treat for you, you just have to work for it."

I watched as his penis grew 3x larger than it was, and the severity of the situation began to set in. This was actually happening.

"Don't worry I know all these guys," she said to me as she stood behind me still. "You're going to love this."

With that, his cock slid through the hole. It wasn't the biggest, it was about 6 inches long but it was fairly thick. I pulled my head back and it was touching my lip. I was trying to decide whether I should go through with this or not, when the man on the other side decided to make a decision for me. He grabbed the chain and pulled me into the wall, and with that, I was now officially a glory hole cock sucker.
I could taste his precum soaking the inside of my mouth

and he held me in place with the chain and slid his cock in and out of my mouth. While this was going on, my girlfriend decided to slide a lube covered butt plug up my ass.

Suddenly I was feeling extremely turned on by all of this. I no longer stayed in place as this man fucked my mouth.

I began to bob up and down on his thick piece of meat, licking all around the tip, feeling the shape of his cock with my mouth. I could feel the little drips of precum oozing out. Eventually he began to make some noise behind the wall and I could feel his cock began to fatten up inside of my mouth. He moaned as he reached his breaking point, and with that, he exploded inside of my mouth.

His cum tasted much worse than mine. He must've not cum in a while, so I immediately spat out the big load onto my chest much to the chagrin of my girlfriend, who was still in the stall with me. She immediately scooped it up and put it back into my mouth.

"Swallow it down sissyboy!" she said. "A good cock sucker doesn't waste a drop!"

After all of that, I asked her if we could go, saying that

I had done it and didn't mind it.

"Oh you're not going anywhere," she said as I heard another man walk into the adjacent stall. "Right on time," she said as I heard his pants drop to the floor.

I looked through the glory hole and saw that this guy was already pretty hard. His cock was also much smaller than the last guys, which was a bit of a relief considering my jaw was a bit sore. It was about 5 inches long, but not nearly as thick.

His cock slid through the hole and I immediately took it into my mouth. It tasted pretty good actually, much better than the last guy. I licked all around his tip and felt some precum in my mouth. I felt my cock dripping precum all over my thighs, just below my plugged ass. It was out of reach though, as I was stilled handcuffed.

I kept sucking on this guy, licking his tip and twirling my tongue around his shaft. Eventually he pulled back and I looked through to see him rubbing himself really fast. I opened my mouth and put it up to the hole just in time for him to slide his ejaculating cock back through and into my mouth.

I felt multiple ropes get shot into my mouth, but this time it seemed way less gross. I'm not sure if his load was better, or if I was just becoming a cock slut.

My girlfriend saw that he had cum and grabbed my chin and pulled it up so I was looking at the ceiling.

"Swallow it down," she said as I obeyed, now with much less resistance. "Wow you really do enjoy this don't you?"

With that, the guy in the next stall left and I heard another person enter. I thought there must've been a line or something because that was quick. I looked through and this time, I saw that it was fairly chubby white guy. He pulled his pants down to reveal his flaccid cock.

"I hope you're ready for this," he said as he slid it on through.

I opened my mouth and wrapped my lips around his tip. Once again, I felt a lot less grossed out about being a glory hole cock sucker. I was still handcuffed, with my face chained to the glory hole, but I didn't feel like I was being forced anymore.

I wanted to do this now. My distraction away from the cock in my mouth was quickly ended when his small, flaccid cock enlarged into a long, fairly thick piece of meat. He was a grower, and as I backed up in awe to get a good look at his beautiful cock, I was interrupted be a gentle tug on the chain.

"I didn't say stop, now get sucking," he said as he tugged on the chain again much harder this time.

I took it all in, and attempted to deepthroat it, but I couldn't handle it. It was just too long and thick. My girlfriend overheard me gagging and laughed.

"Breath through the nose, idiot," she said as she pushed my face into the hole.

After a few more seconds of struggling, I finally figured out how to suppress my gag reflex and deep throat his big cock. There I was, butt filled with a plug, face chained to a glory hole with a big cock head slapping my tonsils around. I was in total bliss. I must've lost track of time, but I swear this big penis was sliding down my throat for a solid 10 minutes.

I was drooling all over the place while this happened. It was amazing. After a while his pace slowed, and I heard him ask if I was ready. I knew what was gonna happen, he slowed down and pulled his cock out all the way except for just the tip. I licked around his peehole when suddenly I felt a thick, tasty rope of cum shoot out into my mouth.

"Mmmmm," I exclaimed as shot after shot of his cum was deposited directly onto my tongue. His load was absolutely massive.

After he filled my mouth completely full with his delicious cum, my girlfriend walked over to tell me to swallow it, but I had already beaten her to it. I'd gulped it all down the second he pulled his cock out of my mouth.

"Wow, you are really enjoying this now aren't you," she quipped.
"Wow, where do you think you're going?" she said "I still have one more guy for you to drain," and with that, I heard the stall open on the other side.

I gazed through the gloryhole for a few seconds before out from the side walked my next cock. He was a very tall black man.

"I saved you the best for last," she said to me with a bit of snicker.

"I hope you're ready for this," he said as I watched on through the glory hole.

With that, he lowered down his gym shorts, very slowly. He kept getting lower and lower and I never saw the end of it, until finally, I saw the tip.

His cock was gigantic. It had to have been over ten inches long! He was already hard too. I looked on in awe for a good 20 seconds before he finally inched closer to the glory hole. Finally, he slid it through and I got a good look.

His cock was extremely thick, fattening up just below the head at its largest point. A perfectly shaped, pink head greeted me face to face.

I noticed a little drop of precum start to form at the end, and with that, I took him into my mouth. I started by licking around his delicious tip, feeling every drop of precum that came out right on my tongue.

I took it in, and felt it get even bigger inside of my mouth. I was enjoying taking it slow when suddenly, my face was once again pushed up to the stall.

My girlfriend was pushing off the other side of the wall, and putting her ass against the back of my head, forcing my face right up to the glory hole. I tried to speak, but my speech was muffled by the behemoth in my mouth.

He must've been in on it cause at this point he went as deep as he could. I was gagging pretty badly but once again tried to suppress my gag reflex and breath through my nose.

So there I was, hands cuffed behind my back, butt plugged, face bound to a glory hole, being held up against the wall as a big black cock slid in and out of my mouth after I had just swallowed 3 loads of cum from other guys. I was having fun. I loved the whole thing. I just relaxed and let him do all the work, my mouth was just a hole for him to use for his pleasure. After about 5 minutes of this, his large black cock suddenly stopped fucking my throat and pulled out so his tip was just inside my lips.

"Try and make me cum, bitch," he said through the stall, as I realized it was my time to start doing some of the work.

He once again pushed his cock all the way through the glory hole, and I backed up a bit and looked at it. A beautiful, pink head topped off the saliva covered cock as it twitched up and down.

I immediately took the tip back in my mouth and bobbed up and down on the first 4-5 inches, wrapping my tongue around it as I sucked.

"MMmmmm fuck yeah," he said from the other stall as his delicious precum leaked out into my mouth.

I kept moving my head up and down, licking everywhere I could. Tonguing his peehole, licking his frenulum, tasting his delicious precum. This went on for another 5minutes before he started moving again. My girl pushed my face up to the stall wall again and he began to throat fuck me once again, this time even harder. I could hear him moaning in pleasure from across the stall, I knew he had to be getting close.

He kept ramming my tonsils with his cock head, making me salivate all over the floor. I was beginning to get impatient though, I had been servicing his cock for at least 15 minutes and my jaw was beginning to get sore.

Right on queue though, he pulled out and told me to finish him off. As he said that, my girl undid the handcuffs behind my back and I immediately started jerking his cock. I rubbed that thing while my lips wrapped wrong his tip and my tongue teased his head. I rubbed and sucked on him for what seemed like a couple of minutes until I could feel him getting ready to cum.

His big head swelled up and got ready to burst. I was finally rewarded with his big load. The first string shot directly down my throat, which I immediately swallowed, the rest sort of oozed out directly onto my tongue, which allowed me to get a good taste of it. I continued to rub it, stirring his load around while pulses of hot cum shot into my mouth. After about 30 seconds or so, he finally pulled away.

I undid the collar around my neck and stood up and looked in the mirror. My chin was completely covered in a mix of saliva, precum and cum. I opened my mouth and saw that it was completely filled with the load I sucked out of the big black cock.

 I gulped it down and immediately reached for my own cock. I rubbed it a few times and a big load just sort of dribbled out of it.
My girlfriend made sure to catch my load in her hand and feed it back to me. I swallowed it down immediately, being the good little cum swallower that I am.

"Well you had fun, didn't you?" She said. "I knew you'd enjoy that but I didn't think I could ever get you to do it just for fun."

I told her that I enjoyed it a lot after the first cock and that I'd definitely do it again. After that I cleaned myself up and snuck out of there, walking past a group of men who I'm pretty sure I'd just sucked off, when one of them slapped me on the ass and winked at me. I had my fun that day and want to go to a glory hole again sometime in the future.

TYPICAL IN-LAWS
Forced with in-laws Story

My wife and I had been married about 25 years when we started thinking about buying some type of vacation home. When my wife's parents heard about our interest, they said that they had a friend who needed to sell a place in the Ozarks really cheap. It sounded like just the kind of place we were looking for. We planned a trip to go see the place as soon as possible. It was to be me, my wife, and my mother and father-in-law.

My in-laws had always been great. I loved being around them. They were both getting up in age, both were around 65. My father-in-law was the typical big bellied gray haired man. Probably pushing 220 pounds. Always kind and considerate. My mother-in-law was his twin. Chubby and huge sagging tits. I had seen her nipples a few times by accident and through her clothes and they really stuck out, at least an inch when she was cold.

My father-in-law, Keith, had gotten detailed directions to the mountain home and a key from his friend. The day before we were to leave, my wife got word that she was needed at work for an audit. She really wasn't that upset as she didn't like long car trips. So it was just the three of us.

We left early Monday morning on our voyage with the goal of spending only one night in a motel. We arrived late at a

Motel 6 and got only one room. Sharing a room was not new for us as we had done this on many trips with them before. I think the in-laws had long stopped having sex.

The next morning, we got back on the road and were soon in the mountains of the Ozarks. The scenery was incredible. My mother-in-law, Helen, was in the back seat having the time of her life. Keith was helping me navigate in the front seat. After we turned off of the main road, we were strictly on dirt back roads with no markings at all. Fortunately, the map we had from the owners was fairly detailed. We were at least 40 miles back in the sticks when we finally reached a cabin perched on the side of a mountain. The view was incredible. The air was clean and cool. We knew that this was the place for us.

The three of us quickly got out and looked the place over. Keith opened the cabin and we went inside. The place had a nice kitchen, two bedrooms and a huge living area. The living area also had a king size bed pushed into one corner.

We had just decided to unpack the car when we were startled by a booming voice from the front door. "What you folks doin here?" We all turned to see a large elderly man wearing overalls standing in the door. He was also holding a shot gun. Keith stepped forward and began, " I'm Keith, this is my wife Helen, and that is our son-in-law, Mark. We're here to look at the cabin. The owners are friends of ours and we're thinking about buying it." The man quickly replied, " I'm the owner of this place, and you folks are trespassin."

I could tell my father-in-law was getting a little nervous as he told man, " I don't think we're in the wrong place, but we will be happy to leave until we can sort this situation out." "I don't need no sortin, you are trespassin. Now the three of ya, back up against the bed." We all moved back against the bed in the living room. The burly grampa then stated,"Now you need to pay for your crime." Me and my father-in-law began reaching for our wallets. "I don't need no money, I want some entertainment. Now all of you strip."

Helen had been very quiet up until this point, but she immediately began protesting and sternly telling the old grandpa that he was out of his mind if he thought we were going to strip. That's when we heard the shot gun being pumped as a shell was readied. We knew at that point he was serious. The three of us slowly began removing our clothes until we were all down to our underwear. I have to say that seeing my in-laws in their underwear was giving me a hard on, just when I didn't need one. "Off with the rest of it, NOW!" our captor shouted. At this point I noticed he had lowered the shot gun and his hand was reaching inside his overalls past his huge belly. I knew he was rubbing that old grandpa cock.

We all slowly removed our underwear. To my surprise, Keith was also showing signs of a hard on. The foreskin on his old uncut cock was beginning to slide back just a bit as I watched him lower his boxers. It was no use hiding my hard cock.

It was at full staff as I dropped my underwear and everyone in the room was looking at it. I didn't think I could get any harder until I turned to see my mother-in-law uncovering those 44ddd tits. Her nipples were sticking out at least an inch, with huge saucers behind them. She then leaned over to pull down her panties. That is when I saw the most beautiful hairy cunt I have ever seen. It was incredible and she knew every male in the room was looking at her pussy. I could almost smell her cunt.

Our grandpa captor then ordered the three of us onto the bed, with Helen to be in the middle. "Boys, each of you take a tit and suck it", we were instructed. I didn't like being in this situation, but I had always wanted to suck her tits. Keith and I both took a tit in our mouths and began sucking. Helen was very rigid at first, but I could tell she was beginning to get aroused just like the rest of us. Her breathing was beginning to speed up as we sucked on those hard erect nipples.

I soon heard, "Hey son-in-law, keep suckin that tit, but you need to reach over and stroke your daddy-in-laws cock." I had never ever touched another man's cock, but I realized I really wanted to stroke Keith's cock. I reached over and began fondling those huge hanging balls and was soon moving my hand up and down on his shaft. All the while sucking Helen's tit. Keith now had a solid hard on and I knew he was enjoying it. I knew it wouldn't be long before one of us would cum, but our captor decided it was time for me to change position. "Keith, you keep sucking that tit, but son-in- law, get between her legs and lick that cunt and asshole."

My mature mother-in-law slowly spread her legs as I release suction on her nipple and repositioned myself between her legs. Her pussy smelled so good. It was powdered and very hairy. I slowly began to lick up and down on her slit and it quickly began to open for me revealing a wet pink interior. Her pussy juice was heaven. I buried my tongue into her as deeply as I could. She softly began moaning as her tit was being sucked and her pussy stimulated. Her clit became aroused and sprang up about a half inch. I responded by sucking on it like it was another nipple. Just when I got into a good pattern of licking, Grandpa ordered me to start on her asshole. I had to get my hands under her thighs and lift them so that I could gain access to her rosebud. It was already wet from the licking and pussy juice that was leaking out. My tongue began circling her opening and then pushing deeper as it relaxed and opened.

 I could see Keith's cock was throbbing as I know he could hear the slurping I was doing on his wife. She was actually squealing as my tongue was in as deep as I could push it into her asshole. I thought I would cum any second as I experienced the smell and sounds of rimming my 65 year old mother-in-law.

Our Grandpa captor had other plans though. "Boy, you want to fuck your mamma-in-law?", He knew that I did and I knew that Helen was ready. Grandpa order Keith to lay on his back and for Helen to begin sucking him. My mother-in-law then revealed that she had never sucked a cock and wasn't about to start. My pour father-in-law had never had his cock sucked. Our captor, though, told her bluntly, " you either suck his or you suck mine". She slowly began licking and bobbing on Keith's hard cock. "Now son-in-law, move in behind her and fuck her doggy style". I was ready. My cock slid in with no resistence. I think it startled her a little as my cock appeared to be about 2" longer than Keith's. I had entered a virgin region of her pussy and she was loving it. Keith was also about to cum as I noticed the strained look on his face. I couldn't take anymore and began slamming my cock hard into my mother-in-law. She stopped sucking Keith to scream and I saw stream after stream of my father-in-laws cum pump onto her face. I buried my cock deep into her cunt and held it there as I pumped a full load of cum into her cunt. She was licking the cum off of her face as I finished squirting the last drops into her warm pussy.

I was slowly pulling out when I heard a noise behind me. I turned to see our Grandpa captor stepping out of his overalls and he was showing the thickest cock I have ever seen. He really was as thick as a beer can. Not very long, but I don't think I could have put my hand completely around it. I could also see the look of surprise on Keith's face as well. Helen was still up on her hands and knees and had no clue that she had another naked man in the room staring at a gaping cunt with lots of cum leaking out of it. Grandpa quietly pulled me aside and aligned his sausage with her cunt. Keith was really getting into watching this old man about rip his wife's pussy apart. Keith looked at me shook his head as if to say, let him do it. I moved aside and watched as the tip of the old cock was rubbed against her soaking pussy lips. She still thought it was me playing with her as she began rock back against the old man's cock. His cock was finally wet enough the he began pushing in and penetrating and stretching her pussy walls.

 He was about half way in when she realized that something was different. Just as she turned her head to see what was happening, Grampa forced his sausage all the way in. Helen screamed both from the size of the cock inside her and from seeing that it was our captor now fucking her. She didn't know quite what to do as she looked at Keith for guidance. Keith just smiled and said, "You have to let him fuck you".

Keith and I both saw the shot gun laying on the floor, but neither of us was interested in stopping what we were doing. Seeing his wife fucked a second time had given Keith and me raging hard ons again. My father- in-law reached over and began stroking my cock as he led me onto the bed next to where his wife was being stretched and fucked. She was really enjoying herself at this point as she was rocking onto the huge donkey size cock.

Keith meanwhile had pushed me down and was beginning to lick and suck my cock. It was still covered with cum and pussy juice from fucking his wife. He seemed to relish the sucking even more as he cleaned my cock and balls. Keith then raised my legs and began licking my asshole. I had never had this done to me by anyone. What an incredible feeling. I'm not sure who was squealing more, me or my mother-in-law.

Keith had stopped licking my asshole but he was still lifting my legs in the air. I was about to be fucked. I didn't know what to think. He was doing this on his own without being forced to by our captor. I was hot and delerious and I wasn't about to stop him. I could feel his cock head massaging the opening of my ass. Then he inched it in ever so slowly. It was a mixture of pain and extreme pleasure and then I could feel his balls and body against mine. He was all the way in. Slowly, he began to pump my ass. He sped up until he matched the rythum of the old man fucking his wife. They both were side by side pumping their own respective pussies. I now knew what women feel when they are being fucked and I liked it. The two old men were continuing to speed up and they were close to emptying their seed. As if it were planned, they both began to jerk. I could feel the warm cum filling my insides. My mother-in-law was screaming like a wild animal. She was cumming harder than she had ever done in her life. Suddenly, my prim and proper mother-in-law was screaming, "fuck me" over and over again. It surprised everyone in the room.

My father-in-law was laying on top of me as he let his cock finish emptying into me. He then stood up slowing pulling out of my ass. Grampa was doing the same as everyone was exhausted from the fuck fest.

The old man then walked over and began dressing in his overalls. "I hope you folks like the place and buy it. Love to do this again sometime". With that, he grabbed his shot gun and left.

My in-laws were very quiet as we dressed and left for home. We had driven for about an hour when my mother-in-law said, "We need to buy this place and come back". Keith looked at me and winked as we both knew that our sex lives were about to dramatically improve.

SUZANNE
Forced Submission Story

Suzanne was taking a long hot shower after a day of visiting with old friends and business meetings. She was staying in a hotel near the airport in a city she new only too well.

It was 10PM when Suzanne stepped from the shower to dry herself. She watched herself in the mirror as she touched her soft moist body. She wrapped the towel around herself and proceeded to the bed to watch some TV.

As she excited the bathroom, Suzanne was grabbed from behind and thrown to the bed face down. The man pushed her head hard to the mattress, "Keep Quiet and you won't be harmed."

Suzanne tried to resist and cry out, but he was much too strong as he wrestled her arms behind her back. "Another sound and you will be gagged."

He quickly handcuffed her wrists behind her back, then blindfolded her. Suzanne lay there almost naked, helpless at the hands of a man she could not see.

The man slapped her towel covered ass, "Pay close attention, and do exactly I say."

Suzanne felt his hands on her ankles as he applied the

leather restraints to each leg. She felt the weight of his body on her as he worked on her leather wrist restraints.

"Spread your legs."

Suzanne lay there horrified, unable to move.

"Spread your legs, now!"

He pulled the towel from her body and slapped her on the ass hard, "I am not going to tell you again."

This time, hesitantly, Suzanne complied. She felt his knee between her legs tight up against her ass.

"Just relax, I'm going to remove the metal cuffs."

Slowly, he unlocked her right wrist and then the left. He grabbed her right leg and pulled it back to fasten her wrist cuff to her ankle.

He repeated the process with the left. She lay there, totally naked, face down with her legs spread wide and unable to move.

Suzanne squirmed as she felt his hands on her ass. She felt her ass cheeks being forced apart and his finger just inside of her wet pussy.

"Nooooo," Suzanne cried no as she felt his finger go deeper.

He quickly removed his finger, "Be quiet, or you will be punished for the outburst."

Suzanne felt the sharp sting of a leather whip slap across her ass cheeks.

"Ow, ohm, please, please nooooo," she whispered.

"No?"

"Pleeeease..." as she felt another sharp sting.

Again, Suzanne felt her ass cheeks being pulled apart and a cold liquid dropping, then running down the crack of her ass.

"Just relax, I am going to insert a small plug in your ass. If I feel any resistance, I will fuck that tight little asshole, understand?"

"Yes," she whimpered.

Suzanne lay there totally helpless, at his mercy as he slid the plug in slowly.

She tried to relax, but it was too big. He continued to push it slowly until it was all the way in.

"Good girl," he said as he rubbed her red ass softly where the whip had previously landed.

"I think you need a reward," he said as he turned the vibrating plug on high.

"Ohhh..."

Suzanne submissiveness was starting to take control as she tried to fight the feeling of arousal, but she could feel his hands between her legs working their way up to her helpless pussy. She felt his fingers tugging and pulling her labia apart. He massaged her pussy with great patience and she could feel herself getting wet and her little clit getting hard.

Suzanne felt her lips being parted with a cold object.

"Hold still, these are called Ben WA balls."

One at a time she felt her lips being parted as he pushed them deep inside with his fingers. When both were inside she felt his fingers moving inside her and the balls would click and vibrate together. If she could of, she surely would of pushed her hips against his fingers, but Suzanne still lay there at his mercy.

Suzanne felt his fingers being pulled out slowly, very slowly. He removed his wet fingers and rubbed them on Suzanne's lips for her to taste.

"Very nice," he told her as she licked and sucked her own juices from his fingers.

As Suzanne lay there, she could her him getting undressed. She tried to struggle, but the restraints were just too tight. She was his for the taking.

Suzanne felt his hands on the inside of her thighs, barely touching, almost to the point of tickling. She could feel his fingers moving upwards slowly, then her lips being pulled apart. Suzanne then felt the heat of his breath on her wetness.

"Stop, please... please?"

Suzanne could feel the heat of his tongue as it plunged in and out of her wet pussy. And quickly as he has started, he had stopped.

"I can see that you like this. Your pussy is soaking wet."

Just then, she felt her labia being teased by an intense vibration, then felt her lips being forced apart and a small object sliding deep within her.

"Do you like this toy? It's just a small vibrating egg."

"Yess, oh, yes..."

He walked around the bed and grabbed her hair, "If you obey me, I will remove the restraints. If you disobey me, your punishment will be severe, understand?"

"Oh yes."

He pulled her head over to the edge of the bed, then walked around behind her and between her legs.

Again she felt the vibration. This time it was deeper, much deeper. She could feel the Ben Wa balls clicking together as the vibrating egg was set to high.

Suzanne felt him press on her plug hard, then slapped her on the ass. He walked around in front of her and grabbed her head.

"I want you to suck my cock."

Suzanne hesitated, then felt the sting of the whip hitting her ass and her tender lips.

"Suck my cock!"

Suzanne opened her mouth and the man guided his massive cock between her soft lips. She sucked the head of his throbbing member, then he pulled away.

She licked his pre-cum, then took his gift as he fucked her face. Suzanne moaned as the vibration between her legs became more intense.

Suzanne felt the steady whipping across her ass and on her pussy.

"Suck harder!"

She could feel herself starting to cum as the small leather straps struck her ass and her swollen pussy lips. The vibration deep in her pussy, the egg causing the Ben Wa balls to click together and in her ass, the vibrating plug deep inside was just too much for her to handle. She tried to cry out, but the man forced his cock deep down her throat. She had taken him completely.

Suzanne squirmed as the man pulled out and squirted all over her face.

"Stop, stop, pull it out, ohhhh, my ..."

Suzanne felt her flood gates open like never before.

"Please, shut it off! Pleeeease?"

With that, he reached over her and shut off both of the toys. Suzanne lay there totally drained, still shaking from her intense orgasm.

Suzanne felt the large plug in her ass slowly being withdrawn. "Ohhhhh."

Then the egg being pulled out by the cord. "Ahhhhh."

"Now relax, we have to get the Ben Wa balls." Suzanne felt his fingers entering her sopping wet pussy. He probed deeper and deeper reaching for the elusive balls.

"Ohhh, ahh, no, nooooo."

"I almost have them, just a little deeper."

"OH, Fuck, ohhhhh, you are gonna make me cum again!"

"There we go, good girl, as he pulled them free."

"Oh my Gawd, oh shit, ohhhh," Suzanne said, still shaking.

He slowly removed her restraints. One at a t time, taking care and massaged each wrist and ankle. as she lay there exhausted.

He rolled her over slowly and removed the blindfold, then kissed her deeply on the lips.

Suzanne's fantasy with play rape was complete and without the use of her safe word.

What other fantasies were hidden behind those beautiful eyes?

I would like to invite you to read another one of my books that I think you will really enjoy.
The book is called:

"EXPLICIT DADDY'S ADULT:
Filthy Hot Stories In Family VOL.4"

Enjoy!

WARM PLEASURE
Forced Impregnation Sub Story

He had been tracking his female's scent for days when he located her. Immediately he recognized who she was and what she meant to him. It had taken him awhile to realize that the circling path she was wondering could only mean that she was lost. Amazing, he had never known any of their kind to be lost. She was obviously young. Panic had struck him for a moment that she would be too young. However further study of her scent established her age to be well into her breeding years.

As he had gotten closer to her he could smell her fear when she realized she was being tracked and was running from him. The beast in him gloried at the chase. He had gotten his first look at her when she entered the clearing. She was so small and delicate looking. Surely he had been mistaking, fate surely would not have picked such a creature for one such as he.

He had almost stopped for one breathtaking moment just to fill his eyes with her. He had waited so long for her and now she was but a moment away. When she spotted him she raced for the cover of the trees. He stopped for a second and raised his nose in the air and reveled at her smell. No power on earth could stop him from surging towards her.

He grabbed her hard from behind slamming them both

against a large and unyielding tree. The moment he had touched her, he knew that she was his and he would not be letting her go. He pinned her between himself and the tree. She was trembling and he could smell her fear. He did not like her being afraid of him. He was meant to protect her. But he understood that until she accepted him as her master, her fear of him would help control her.

He began whispering soft words of assurance in her ear. Ever so softly he pulled her long flowing hair from her nape. Still murmuring softly he bent down and pulled the scent of her neck through his nostrils. With small soft strokes of his tongue he lapped gently at her neck. He started suckling on her tender skin leaving possessive red welts along her neck, collar bone, and fragile jaw.

Suddenly a blinding pain wracked his ribs as she struck him with her elbow. He doubled over as she whipped away from him. His arm jerked out and grabbed her arm.

She tried to twist from him but fell. She landed on her back and immediately sprang into a sitting position. He snarled his displeasure at her attempts to escape him. He glared down at her angling his head he emitted a low and menacing rumble from deep in his chest. She started scooting backwards away from him like a crab, afraid to turn her back towards him.

As she moved he stared at her face for the first time. She was stunning. She had a heart shaped face with full red lips that were shaped for kissing and sucking a man's cock. Yes, sucking his cock. Her dark blue eyes that were almost too big for her face, were fringed with dark eyelashes. Her eyebrows were dark blond, several shades darker than her hair. Most of the soft waiving locks cascaded down her back while some spilled over her shoulder and curled around her breast. His gaze slid from her face to her breast. As though they had a mind of their own he could see them swell. They were small like her, but they would be enough for him to enjoy. The nipples hardened and he could see them through her dress. Dark red like berries, begging him to suckle them. He felt his cock go rock hard and before he could stop it a low growl of rolled from him. This time in pleasure.

"My family will come for me." Her voice matched her appearance, soft and delicate. He had no doubt that her family would come for her. In all his travels over the span of two millennia he had never scented one such as her. She must be very rare.

"Let them come. It will nae matter." He stepped towards her. The sooner she accepted that she was his, the better.

He wondered if she already had a male somewhere. If she did, he would enjoy killing him.

Fierce possessiveness rolled through him. Something of his thoughts must have passed over his face because she gave a startled cry. She lunged from her back onto her knees and tried to spring into a run. He lunged forward and grabbed her ankle's. He pulled her legs back towards him. Dragging her face down onto the soft grass. Using his body to keep her down he slowly moved up over her back.

He shifted enough above her so he could rip her dress from her leaving only her sweet ass encased in lacy white panties. He began touching her and stroking her every inch from her heels up to the back of her neck and back down again. His tongue swirled tracing imaginary symbols along her velvet skin. She quivered and tried to move away from him and the sensations he was creating in her young body.

"Let me go and I will not tell." She tried to bargain with him when her struggles did not gain her release but seemed to excite him even more.

"You willnae have to tell them, because I will." He growled in her ear. With one hand he pushed on her lower back trapping her on the ground and with the other hand he twisted her hair in his fist and pulled her head back. He growled has he bit the left side of her exposed neck. He flexed his jaw lightly sinking his teeth around her jugular vein until she stilled. He began to nudge her thighs apart using his strength to keep her pinned.

"I willnae let you see any of them again until your belly is swollen with my seed and your spirit is submitted to me."

It took her a moment to understand his words from his heavy accent. When their meaning penetrated her mind she began to cry and thrash wildly under his heavy frame. He heard her gasp when she realized he meant to take her right there.

"Shh, I wish to taste you." She started to struggle harder causing him to bite into her soft slim thigh until she stilled. She had struggled longer than most would have and he had been forced to break her skin. The smell of her blood so close to her sex was sending him into a sexual frenzy. He did want not hurt her, but she must learn not to deny him.

He started speaking to her in a low melodic voice. Trying to calm her he moved slow and gentle. His body was screaming for him to take her hard and fast. But, his mind was warning him of how soft and delicate she was how easy he could hurt her young womb.

Her scent swirled around him reminding him of how rare she was. Her family must have treated her as the most special of all creatures. But, they had left her unprotected. Something he would never do. She would be his, he would never let her from his site. The only way she would be away from his site was if she had to take a piss. Hell, he didn't mind watching his woman piss, on second thought he could think of no reason for her to be away from his side.

He pushed her legs wide enough apart to allow his mouth to lick at the satin crotch of her small lace panties. A low growl of approval escaped him as he scented her innocence. He could feel her tremble as his tongue warmed her through her panties. Her small body tensed trying to override the pleasurable sensation.

Her breast began to swell and feel heavy. She could not seem to stop herself fro grinding her tender nipples into the dirt. She heard a noise that sounded like an animal in need. It stunned her to realize the sound was coming from her. She groaned with humiliation at the though that she had no control over her body.

His tongue began to lap at her growing wetness through her panties. One hand held tightly to her slim thigh while the fingers of his other hand began to press rhythmically into her tight pussy. She could feel her blood pulse in between her legs. With every heartbeat his fingers would push her panties slightly into her warm wet pussy.

He removed his fingers from her dripping panties and she let out a low keeling noise. His fingers started tracing the edge of her panties. She could not stop herself from lifting her bottom in the air to give him better access. She could not help but submit to the pleasures that he was forcing on her. Laying on her stomach thrusting her ass in the air she trembled with anticipation.

Her scent of arousal and submissive movements through him into a frenzy and he grabbed her hips jerking them back higher into the air. His canines lengthened and he buried his face in her ass and chewed through her panties to get to her tiny puckered hole. Suckling and nipping at her tiny rose bud he began to thrust his tongue deep inside her sweet little pucker while hand moved to stroke her pussy.

His thumb dipped into her tight little channel while his fingers surrounded her little pleasure bud pressing them in matching rhythm to his tongue.
She could not believe what he was doing. No one in her young life had ever touched her this way. Tears of pleasure

and embarrassment streaked her face as she could not stop herself from enjoy his fingers on her clit and his tongue in her bottom. She felt him shift slightly. Fearing that he meant to stop she grabbed both her ass cheeks and stretched them as far apart as she could and pressed her ass back against his mouth. She heard him chuckle his delight at her movements and could not help but contain the sudden blush at how happy this made her.

Her thighs began to tremble and a knot began to form low in her belly and her lower back. She wasn't expecting the sudden surge of complete pleasure but suddenly her hands flew from her body and grabbed handfuls of grass as she screamed and writhed on his tongue. Gasping and shuddering she fell limp on the ground.

Softly he moved up to her and gently moved the tangled mass of her plastered on her soft cheek.

"We are not done yet little one." His voice seemed to come from his chest and she couldn't help but press her back against his chest while she purred.

Gently yet forcibly he rolled her onto her back. His claws extended and he tore away the remaining shreds of her lace panties. Positioning himself between her thighs, he knelt there and stared at her naked beauty.

Her body was still limp with her previous orgasm, she offered no resistance as he positioned her as he wanted her.

Slipping his left arm under her butt cheeks he lifted her up where only her shoulders and head rested on the grass. He ran his right hand between her breast, up stroking her neck and collarbone, and then down again pressing hard as he traveled past her ribs onto her stomach. He pressed harder just under her belly- button and she felt her womb jump. Her body already recognizing its master. He smiled as he stoked her and let loose a shear growl of pleasure when he felt her tiny womb jump at his touch.

He slowly lowered her down on the ground and low between her thighs. Using his large hands he splayed her thighs wide while stretching her pussy lips tightly almost painfully apart. Her delicate little clit stood unprotect and bare to his visual examination.

"Don't." She tried to cover herself but a warning growl from him scarred her enough to lay back and be still for him. He bent his head down low and blew across her little clit watching her body jump at the sudden sensation.

At first she felt him touch her exposed clit only with his lips. It was so soft and subtle she sighed. He began to pull her clit into his warm wet mouth with long drawn suckling motions. His wet tongue began to dip into her little cunny and swirl her growing juices out and suck them off her little pleasure button. Her head began to thrash and her skin felt like it was on fire. His fingers released her pussy lips and began to stroke her. He raised up licking her scent off his mouth as he watched her through heavy lids.

She moaned and moved as his fingers pressed and stroked her. She couldn't believe what was happening. She tried to get control of herself and close her legs. A shout of anger erupted from him and his fingers became painful.

"I told you, do not deny what is mine." She struggled to understand his words as his fingers pressed hard into her forcing both pain and pleasure upon her young body. Suddenly without mercy, he pressed hard into her clit. The pressure caused and instant orgasm to roll through her. Unlike the one before though, this one was painful and caused her whole body to clench. She looked up at him with tears in her eyes, innocent and confused.

"I will have what is mine." He pushed his cock just barely into the small opening of her virgin opening.

"You can take it with pain, or with pleasure, but either way you will take it." With these words he shoved his huge cock deep into her virgin cunt. She screamed and bucked at the pain.

He shouted his uncontrollable joy when he ripped through her maidenhead. The realization that no one had ever had her before or would ever have her but him caused his cock to grow and jump in her tight cunny.

"Tell me, who owns you?" He fisted her hair as he jerked back into her. She felt her pussy lips dimple back into her dry pussy as he forced his cock back into her abused little cunny. She began to cry and whimper as he slammed into her cervix. He jerked her hair again and pulled from her only to ram back into her again.

"Tell me, who owns you?" He snarled again.

"You...you do." She gasped as she pushed at his hips trying to ease some of her pain.

"Do you willing accept my seed?" This time she did not wait for him to ask twice.

"Yes...anything." Her body shuddered when he suddenly stopped pistoning into her.

Just as suddenly as he had taken her with force he began moving on her with gentleness. He slowed his thrusts and began stroking her clit with his fingers. He bent his head down and began suckling her nipples.

A shudder raced up her back as he began to arouse her. She felt the wetness grow between her legs with every thrust. Where his cock had felt too big and had hurt before, now she began to arch up towards his thrust, craving the full feeling. His warm mouth sucked and nipped at her breast. He licked his way up to her throat.

"Do you want me to cum in you?" His voice was but a hoarse whisper. She nodded and turned her head to press her lips against his cheek.

She could hear his growls against her throat.

She wrapped her arms around him trying to hold him to her as she felt her pleasure grow. He started rocking her back and forth with each thrust. Her breathing became labored and black dots swam around her head. Through a pleasure filled haze she lifted her head to see where the two of them were joined. The site of his cock sinking into her warm inviting pussy was the most erotic sight she had ever witnessed.

Unable to control the beast in himself anymore he bit into her neck holding her beneath him so his body could fill her with his life giving seed. She felt his teeth sink into her neck but instead of pain she could feel only pleasure. Her body began to prepare itself for the best orgasm of its young life as she began to beg him to finish her off.

She felt him release her neck as he threw his head back and roared up to the sky. Her body exploded as her pussy clamped down on his cock milking him as his hot seed bathed her womb.

Slowly their breathing began to turn back to normal.

The realization of what just occurred hit her and she began to weep. Slowly their breathing began to turn back to normal. The realization of what just occurred hit her and she began to weep.

His shirt and pants were unbuttoned, but for the most part he was completely clothed, while she was totally naked. She felt scarred and insecure.
he starred down at her. She looked so small and fragile lying there beneath him.

"When my family finds me they will kill you for this."

Maybe not so fragile.

He was not afraid of her family but her words reminded him he needed to get back to his homegrown. Only there would he feel safe with his prize. He took his shirt off and helped her into it, buttoning it up himself.

Knowing that she might try to escape or cry out he decided he would quiet her. "I am going to quiet you." Straddling her back he started to tear the skin from his index finger. Her she growled a small feral sound that made him get rock hard again. Then she started gnashing at him with her teeth. Little minx meant to bite him.

He grabbed a handful of hair with his left hand to keep her head still. Then he grasped her jaw with his right. He put his thumb on one side of her face and using every finger but his index finger he grasped the other side of her jaw.

This way he could apply pressure to both sides of her jaw should she decide to bite him. He tried to force his bleeding finger into her mouth but she would not open her mouth. He was afraid to apply to much pressure less he hurt her.

"You can either take my blood into your wee little body, by your mouth." He waived his bloody finger in front of her eyes and waited for a moment to heighten the shock of his next words. "Or I can shove it in your tight little sheath, and you can take it that way."

Her reaction was instant and just what he had wanted. Her eyes popped open and her small mouth opened into a perfect "Oh!" As she gasped in shock. He immediately pushed his finger into her warm mouth. As his blood started pulling there she had no choice but to swallow.

As soon as she did her eyes began to flutter. Small little noises escaped her as she began to suck and pull the blood from his wound. He would not have been a male if he could not resist lowering himself to her.

He spoke tender words of praise and pleasure in her ear. He used the tone of his voice to reassure her as she began to grow lethargic at the taste of his blood. Rubbing her with his body, he began the age old dance of his kind as he marked her with his scent.

"You have taken both my blood and my seed. You are mine little one." As her eyes began to flutter close the last thing she remembered was him pressing a kiss onto her belly before lifting her up into his arms and heading towards his home.

OFFICE BLACKMAIL
Forced Bdsm Story

She straightened her clothes and washed her hands, then flushed the toilet for good measure before pushing open the bathroom door and running headlong into her boss. By his casual stance, she knew he'd been standing there waiting for her to emerge. She could feel her face flushing, but there was no way he knew what she was doing in the bathroom.

He smiled down at her and placed a gentle hand on her shoulder. "I think we should take a walk," he said in a way that suggested she didn't have a choice in the matter.

Fear sluiced through her in that moment; anytime he took someone for a walk, it was a prelude to the person being terminated. She'd already had one hell of a year with her husband walking out on her and divorcing her to marry his pregnant girlfriend. His very young, very sexy girlfriend. Debby's hair was blonde only through the magic of Clairol, whereas her ex-husband's girlfriend was half their age and didn't have to cover any grey.

Debby kept the house and her car, but finances have been so tight that she's been on the verge of losing everything for months. She had no idea what she'd do if she lost her job on top of everything else. And she knew if Mr. Daniels terminated her she wouldn't be eligible for unemployment.

She followed him in silence as he quickly led her down the hall to his office. His office sat at the far end of the building, away from the cubicles where she worked, and even from the offices of the other executives. Mr. Daniels was not only the managing executive, but he was the founder and CEO.

She was just a data entry clerk.

"Route my calls to Alex and let him know what's going on. Once you've done that you may take your lunch," he told his office assistant without breaking stride. He opened the door to his office and ushered Debby inside, then closed it behind both of them.

Mr. Daniels walked behind his desk and sat in his oversized leather desk chair and pointed at the small wooden stool in front of his desk. "Have a seat, if you will," he offered in a way that also suggested she shouldn't argue.

She shifted around on the stool as if trying to find a comfortable way to sit. Finally, she hooked her legs around either side of the stool's legs and straightened her spine to help her remain upright. The stool's height was so short as to only allow her head to reach the top of the desk's surface. If the stool was meant to intimidate someone, or make them feel inferior, she thought, it was doing a great job.

"Look at me Debby," he instructed her. Looking at him meant craning her neck upwards at an uncomfortable angle, but she didn't have much choice. She was nervous enough about losing her job that she'd do anything now to save it. Too bad she hadn't thought of that sooner.

"Y-yes, sir?" she asked in a quiet, trembling voice.

"Debby, do you know why I've brought you here?" She'd always hated that question. She was being forced to incriminate herself. She normally kept her nose clean and stayed out of trouble, but it was a difficult question to answer. "And before you say no, you should think about it. Think hard about where you just were and why you disappear to the restroom frequently throughout your shift."

Embarrassment flushed her skin bright red. "Umm. Yes, sir," she answered after a long silence. When she would have turned her head down to look toward her lap, her boss made a clucking sound.

"No. You'll keep your eyes on mine until I tell you otherwise, do you understand?" he asked her. She nodded her head in understanding. "Now I understand that you've made a habit of spending a lot of time in the bathroom the past several months. Is there a medical condition of which I should be aware?"

She didn't think she could be any more embarrassed than she already was; she was wrong. "Ahem. Umm. Yes, sir. I mean, no. No, sir."

He tilted his head to the side slightly, as if he were humoring her. "Well which is it? Is there or isn't there?" By the way he asked, it was as if he already knew the answer.

"What I mean sir is that yes, there is. But no, it's not something I should share with you," she said while squirming in the stool. Unhooking her legs from the legs of the stool she made to stand up but her boss shook his head and pointed back at the stool. She tried to find another comfortable position but it seemed even more of a struggle than before.

"As your supervisor," nevermind that there were several levels between the two of them, "it is your responsibility to inform me of any conditions that might impact your performance. As I see it, your work performance has decreased significantly over the past six months, to the point that your continued employment here is no longer guaranteed." He looked at her pointedly, assuring her that her worst fears were about to be realized. "Now I suggest you let me know what's going on so we can find a solution that works for both of us. Hmm?"

"But sir, I ..." she started, clearly not intending to give him the answers he demanded.

He reached for a folder with her name on it and pushed it toward her side of the desk. "Very well, Debby. You've really not left me with a choice. If you aren't able to work with me, I have no choice but to end your employment effective immediately. I'll have someone escort you to your cubicle where you can take any personal belongings." He picked up his phone, pushed an extension and said, "Please have Debby White's final check and exit papers ready within 30 minutes."

Tears came to her eyes and she stood quickly, looking down at Mr. Daniels. "Sir, please don't do this. I'm ... I'll work extra hours without pay to make up any lost time. I'll do whatever is necessary but please. Please, sir, I really need this job." His response was to point at the stool.

"I didn't tell you to stand." She sat again, but this time she sat so far forward on the stool that it nearly toppled over.

"Scoot back, Debby. Sit the stool completely and prepare to talk. Now is your final chance. You have less than one minute."

She waited for a few seconds, then took a deep breath and closed her eyes. This time, he didn't remind her to look into his. "Sir, I'm what people call a nymphomaniac. I can't control myself or my sexual urges. It's a medical condition called Persistent Sexual Arousal, or PSA. It's become much worse since my divorce because I don't have anyone to give me relief after work or at home. I have to go to the bathroom to masturbate so I don't orgasm at my desk." Her humiliation peaked when she heard him chuckle. Tears began to fall freely, and then her body tensed.

"Don't you dare stand," he ordered her in a stern voice, as if anticipating her move. "And open your eyes. I never gave you permission to look away from me," he added.

She opened her eyes and looked at him, an almost pleading expression in her eyes. "You may not move from your spot and you will maintain eye contact with me," he informed her. "Now that you've told me the truth, we can work on a solution that we'll find mutually acceptable." He maintained his stern visage.

"Sir, if I don't stand ..." she left the sentence unfinished, looking into his eyes with a pleading expression.

"What will happen if you don't stand?" he asked, a grin making its way to his face, letting her know that he understood her situation. "You must explain to me what's happening, or what will happen, if I'm to help you."

"The pressure of the stool. I have to stand." Her words were said quickly, somewhat breathlessly.

"Why?" he asked. "Be specific."

One of her hands moved her skirt so that it wasn't in between her and the stool, then both hands gripped the desk in front of her. Though she remained seated and didn't turn her eyes away, she was past the point of being able to speak. Her hips moved back and forth against the stool and she moaned quietly with the orgasm that was quickly approaching. Her eyes closed for just a moment as her breathing quickened. She didn't realize Mr. Daniels was on the move until he put his hands under her arms and pulled her from the stool.

"Girl," he growled. "I did not give you leave to orgasm, especially not on my stool." He pointed at the stool and the thick puddle of her juices. One of his hands slid under her skirt and up her thigh. "Only sluts go to work without wearing panties under their skirts. Lick your juices from the stool."

Debby was stopped just before the orgasm exploded, leaving her on edge and in pain. When she opened her mouth to speak, Mr. Daniels shook his head. "The only thing you'd better be saying right now is thank you. Clean the stool and we'll talk." He kept his eyes on her but moved back around to his side of the desk to open a drawer.

Left without a choice, Debby leaned over the stool and began to lick her juices from it. As sexually heightened as she still was, the action did nothing to diminish her need. She moaned in ecstasy as she tasted herself.

Still bent over the stool, she heard her boss approach her again, but couldn't see what he was doing. He pushed her skirt up to her waist, then pulled both arms behind her and tied them together with something that felt like a rough rope. With her arms positioned thusly, it kept her skirt well out of the way.

"Good. Now that my stool is clean, you can turn around and do the same to my cock." As he turned her around, she noticed that his trousers had been unzipped and his cock was freed from his boxers. It had been a while since she'd been around a cock, and this one was much larger than her husband's, but she knew immediately what to do with it. Without hesitation, she licked her boss' balls hungrily, and even gently sucked them into her mouth. Popping them out of her mouth, she slid her wet tongue up his cock.

Only when his entire length was wet from her tongue did she slide the head of his cock into her mouth.

"Mmmm," she moaned with contentment as he pushed his length into her mouth and toward her throat. He wrapped his hands in her hair and pulled her mouth closer to his crotch, not even bothering to stop when he knew the tip of his cock was hitting the back of her throat.

"Yes, that's a good girl," he whispered encouragingly. "Swallow and you'll take it in better," he instructed her. He only stopped pushing when his balls were resting on her chin, but he held it for a few seconds longer than he knew was comfortable. "Look up at me," he ordered her.

Her eyes looked up at his, and even though her arms were tied behind her back and he was using her mouth for his own pleasure, he could see the gratitude shining. "Yes, that's a nice look for a slut like you," he told her. She hummed with him in her throat, and when she saw his eyes widen with the sudden pleasure of it, she tightened her throat muscles to grip him even more tightly. "Oh god," he exclaimed, holding her head so tightly to him that she could barely breathe. Eventually he gained control of himself and released his grip.

"What a nice little slut you are," he grinned down at her once he was able to speak again. "I think I'm going to like your new position and title," he said with a smirk, then pulled out of her mouth. "Since you're not a fan of talking, I thought I'd help you out a bit." He grabbed a ball gag from the desk and forced it into her mouth. "There we go. Good sluts should always have something in their mouth," he informed her. "Now, go ahead and lean over your stool. Your tits should be hanging off. Later, we'll do something about your work uniform, but we'll leave it alone for today." He pushed her over the stool in the position that worked best for him.

"Now, I know your arms are tied behind your back and you've got a gag in your mouth so you can't speak, but I won't have anyone saying that you're an unwilling partner. Go ahead and nod your head in agreement that you're not only willing, but you're eager for me to fuck you." She nodded her agreement before he'd finished speaking.

Moving behind her, he placed one hand on her ass and used the other hand to guide his cock into her pussy. She was wet. Hers was probably the wettest pussy he'd ever explored, and the fact that he was riding her bareback made it all that much better.

"Oh god," were the only words he could exclaim as he buried himself balls deep into her tight pussy. How a slut like her could have such a tight pussy didn't make sense, but it didn't matter. At the moment, nothing mattered but fucking her until they were both senseless. He slid his cock out of her, right to the entrance, then slammed it back into her, forcing her roughly against the stool; the only sound from her was moaning. Her pussy grabbed hold of him tightly and he could feel it pulsing around him, letting him feel her mounting excitement. As aroused as he was, he knew he wouldn't be able to last long.

With one hand still digging into her ass cheek, he slid his other between her legs to find her engorged clit. She twitched when he touched it, so he pinched it between his thumb and forefinger. The louder she moaned, the harder he pinched. He knew she was about to cum so he stopped thrusting. He pinched and rubbed her clit hard and fast until he felt her orgasm overcome her but he didn't stop there. He continued to tease her clit while he resumed thrusting his cock in and out of her. He knew he was taking her up to a second orgasm, but was surprised to feel a third one rip through her in the second before he was ready to blow his own load. Pulling out, he squeezed a load of hot sticky cum on her ass crack before turning her around to bestow the last of it on her face.

"You may not move, slut," he ordered her. Rooting on the top of his desk again, he returned with his phone and took several pictures of her as she was - sexually sated, covered in cum, and looking every bit the slut. "I'm sure your husband's lawyer would love to see these pictures. It's up to you to decide if he ever sees them. I'm going to remove the gag from your mouth long enough for you to clean my cock. If you speak, the pictures will be sent to his lawyer. Do you understand?"

Debby nodded her head. Truth be told, she had so many things swirling around in her mind right now that she didn't think she'd know what to say even if she wanted to. A knock sounded on the office door and she wasn't expecting him to tell the person to enter.

She had a direct view of the door, so she saw her immediate supervisor enter even before he noticed her on the stool.

"Sir, I'm sorry to disturb you, but I ..." and then he noticed her. With a grin, he said "Ahh. I see you've had that conversation we discussed. I'm so glad to see things worked out as well as planned. Is our meeting still on for tomorrow morning, sir?"

While Adam was talking, Mr. Daniels continued what he'd been doing as if nothing were out of the ordinary. He removed the gag from Debby's mouth and placed his cock in front of her lips. "Clean it slut," he said quietly, then nodded to Adam. "Yes, the meeting is still scheduled for tomorrow morning." His cock was growing hard again as it was cleaned. "The conversation went better than anticipated. I might be leaving early today," he admitted with a grin.

CUSTOMER FANTASY
Forced to Make Customer Happy Story

After a long week at work Sara and I were just getting ready to go out for dinner when the phone rang, it was Nicola a wealthy client I had been closely working with for just over a month. She had been so demanding at every little stage of the process and I had been spending a lot of time with her while designing new interiors for her chain of restaurants. Now she was contacting me at home and it would be some insignificant thing that could wait, but she was paying a huge sum of money so I had to bend some rules.

That had meant some late nights at the office in many long meetings with Nicola we had been working closely for about six months. So of course we had got to know much more about each other and had often settled disputes over several bottles of wine. This had led to heated debates about society, ethics and of course sex; which in turn had led Nicola and I share some of our experiences and fantasies.

Nicola was about ten years older than me putting her in her late forties, she was a very fine looking curvy woman, with a lovely firm ass and ample breasts, which she had caught me looking at on more than a few occasions. Nicola's gorgeous voluptuous body was always draped in fine fabrics contouring her hourglass figure and she never failed to wear stylish high heel shoes. Nicola loved to dress in the fifties film star look, teasing people with her stocking tops.

Luckily for me she had clearly taken my lustful stares as compliments and I had noticed she had started to dress even more provocatively each time we met. Showing more cleavage and criminally revealing skirts, taking care to expose her body at every opportunity. There was the day she insisted on climbing the step ladder in her skirt the view of her firm stocking clad legs made me shake as she looked down at me smiling knowing I could see up her shapely legs to her firm thighs.

On the phone Nicola explained there were some changes she wanted to make to my drawings which I had sent over to her today. Nicola was her usual demanding self and said it couldn't wait till Monday and demanded I come over to fix the problem.

Reminding me she was paying for a premium price and that she deserves a premium service.

Sara had heard me say that I would be there in twenty minutes "Oh Lee your joking I thought we we're going out?" moaned Sara as she adjusted her thin tight strapless dress, her pert firm breasts having no trouble holding up the light weight material, Sara's nipples were hard and pushing though the dress, her long black hair cascaded over her shoulders and petite frame.

"Look it will only take a few minutes then we'll carry on to dinner, if your with me it will make her hurry up." I explained and we took a taxi over to Nicola's. Sara clearly wasn't happy but she knew Nicola was a rich important client for me, so I knew Sara would act warmly towards her.

Nicola looked fantastic when she answered the door she had a tight black dress on which showed off her beautiful breasts perfectly. I could see Nicola's smile fade a little when she saw Sara next to me but she greeted us warmly inviting us into her expansive house.

"Hi Nicola this is Sara my wife, we were just leaving for dinner when you rang, so I though I'd introduce her and take a look at the drawings at the same time and then we will go on to dinner". I spoke softly and smiled warmly hoping Nicola would take the hint, that I wanted to be quick.

"Lee you never said you had such s beautiful wife, would you both like a drink?" Nicola offered as she waved us down the hall giving me a frown as she passed by her thin opaque dress clung to her curvy figure I could see suspender straps and the many hooked back of a corset pulling Nicola's waist seductively tight. I was sure she had been planning on something more than just altering the drawings, my mind raced with how I could turn this to my advantage.

Nicola poured large glasses of wine for the three of us and invited Sara to look around the house, while Nicola and I sorted the problem on the drawings.

Sara smiled and thanked her before filling her glass up and walking around the ground floor and gardens of the Nicola's large house. Detouring back through the lounge to fill her glass a couple of time as Nicola and I discussed and debated her changes to the design, which had taken a lot longer than the planned 20 minutes. As I put the drawings away Nicola poured some more wine.

"You have a lovely house Nicola" Sara said as she wandered back into the room walking back through the conservatory. By the look of Sara she had drank a little more wine than I had, as she dainty but unstably climbed the few steps leading up to our level. Sara looked amazing in her high strappy shoes, her thin dress clinging to her body the shape of hips clearly visible as were her still erect nipples.

Nicola showed us into her bedroom which had a huge four poster bed in it "What a fantastic bed I bet you can have some fun on that" Sara exclaimed with a suggestive tone in her voice.

"Get on its really comfy" Nicola said to Sara, Sara climbed into the middle of the bed and flung her arms out.

"Oh my god it's got a mirror above you, hmm very kinky" Sara laughed.

"Well a girls got to have some fun." Nicola replied as she opened a draw in her bedside table and took out some ropes, she threw a couple to me.

"Come on Lee lets show Sara how she should use this bed" I didn't need to be asked twice and grabbed a rope and Sara's hand and slipped the loop that was in the rope over her wrist and pulled it tight, Nicola was doing the same thing.

It took Sara a moment to realise what was happening by this time we had the ropes round the posts of the bed and secured them tightly. Sara was struggling

"Come on let me out please a jokes a joke". Sara asked.

"Sara come on lets just tie your legs up so you get the full effect" I said as Nicola looked at me for permission and we grabbed Sara's ankles putting loops of rope over them and tying them to the bottom posts. Leaving Sara powerless with her legs spread apart, she struggled to get loose but we had tied the ropes to tight.

"Wow that looks so good Sara, we could do anything I wanted to you now" I said.

"Ooh yes she does look sexy like that" Nicola said licking her lips.

"Well why don't you do something to her then Nicola" I said. Sara began to struggle again.

"No Lee just untie me, please don't" Sara pleaded.

Nicola looked over at me: "Go on Nicola do what ever you want to her, she knows she has to obey me" I said as Sara continued to struggled in the ropes. Nicola reached over and felt Sara's breast sliding her hand into Sara's dress and squeezed her nipple Sara shuddered.

I pulled Sara's dress up to her waist and I got a surprise to see she didn't have any underwear on her neatly trimmed pussy looked wonderful her lips glistened with juices. Nicola looked down and smiled.

"Hmm what a dirty bitch! It looks like she was planning to give you a good time tonight" and she reached down to stroke Sara's pussy.

"Right you've had your fun let me go please" Sara asked as she wriggled, I slapped her thigh hard Sara yelped as my hand made contact with her skin

"You know I'm in control so stop moaning and lie there, go on Nicola carry on, Sara will do as she's told" I ordered, Nicola had jumped at the sound of the slap. Nicola smiled and forced two fingers inside Sara's pussy, Sara gasped.

I moved round to where Nicola was standing and unzipped her dress revealing a corset, suspenders and stockings; she looked like a sexy slutty burlesque star.

Nicola pulled her fingers from Sara and licked the juices off them before wriggling out of her dress and took her bra off her large breasts looked so sexy when they swung down as they were released.

"Hmm they look nice" Sara gasped at the sight, as Nicola's breasts were a lot bigger than her own, Nicola turned back to Sara and squeezed her heavy breasts together, she reached over and grabbed Sara's dress and ripped it open from the hem all the way up to the top leaving Sara's naked body exposed.

"My dress" Sara screamed.

Nicola rammed her fingers back into Sara's juicy pussy and knelt on the bed so she could lick her. I pulled Nicola's black lacy panties down taking them right off before gently stroking her wet and juicy pussy, Nicola opened her legs and my fingers slipped easily inside her. In her open drawer I could see a large thick dildo; I lent over and got it out, Nicola looked round.

"Give it to me" she asked I gave it to her and she pushed it firmly into Sara's pussy, Sara moaned with pleasure as Nicola began to rhythmically pump it in and out of Sara.

Kneeling behind Nicola and parted her ass so I could lick her juices as they dripped out of her pussy lips, she moaned some encouragement to me as we shifted position so Nicola and Sara could kiss, Nicola's large breast rubbed against Sara's hard nipples. Nicola's shapely body writhing on top of Sara looked so erotic I thought my cock was going to explode. I moved in between Nicola's legs and slowly sunk my hard swollen cock into her hot pussy.

"Oh yes fuck me hard, while I fuck your slut wife with this dildo" Nicola said as began to ram the dildo deep inside of Sara's cunt, Sara groaned I could tell Nicola was causing Sara a little bit of pain with how rough she was being.

Sara was struggling in her ropes again as she tried to ease the pain although judging by the noise she was making I knew she was enjoying it.

They were passionately kissing through the groans and moans they were both making I looked at Nicola's hand ramming the dildo hard into Sara.

I continued to fuck Nicola's pleasing tight cunt rhythmically increasing the speed and the force the more turned on I got; Nicola's pussy was filling with juices which I could feel dribbling out between my thighs and her ass. My cock getting stiffer and hard as the pressure in my balls built. Nicola shuddered as I shot my hot cum deep inside her, I could feel her cunt pulsate against my cock as she orgasmed.

As I pulled my cock from Nicola I could see our mixed juices as they oozed from her lips, I watched as Nicola moved her head down to Sara's clit and started to lick and nibble it until Sara began to shout "Oh my god oh my god" as an orgasm pulsated through her.

As we untied Sara and she sat up rubbing her wrists smiling and removed her tattered dress, Nicola looked at Sara and said "Right you're going to lick Lee's cum from my pussy" Sara shifted in the bed and Nicola led on her back her large breasts spreading across her chest, Sara lifted one bringing Nicola's nipple to her mouth.

I knelt on the opposite side to Sara and stroked Nicola's free breast with one hand while using my fingers on the other to rub her juices over her clit and pussy.

"Lee there's some more toys and lube in that draw" Nicola said.

I got another thick dildo out and passed it to Sara as she climbed on top of Nicola in a 69 position her mouth immediately dropping onto Nicola's juicy cunt.

"Hmm I can taste Lee's cum all over you, hmm its so nice" Sara gasped from between Nicola's legs.

Nicola had grabbed Sara's hips and pulled her down onto her own greedy tongue. I carefully pushed the other dildo inside Sara as Nicola's lapped at Sara's lips, as her juices flowed out. Nicola's hand took over on the dildo and I opened the lube smearing it over my now erect cock, I also rubbed some into Sara's anus slowly pushing my index finger into her tight ass hole.

Sara asked for the lube and she began to slide her fingers forcefully into Nicola's ass both women were moaning loudly. I knelt nearer to Sara and held her still by pushing her hips further down onto Nicola's face before placing my cock at the entrance to her ass, pushing harder I felt her anus open up as I slid inside.

Sara gasped as my hard cock pulsated in her. I could feel the dildo that Nicola was using to fuck Sara, rubbing through Sara's pussy wall onto the bottom of my cock I thought I was going to cum but managed to hold it. I heard Nicola groan suddenly and her fingers dug in to Sara's thigh as Sara rammed a dildo hard into Nicola's ass, from the way Sara's arm was moving it looked like Nicola's ass was getting the same rough treatment she had given to Sara.

I fucked Sara's ass with long slow deep strokes both women continuing to moan together both sounding on the edge of an orgasm. Sara was the first to cum as she pushed her cunt and ass deeper onto my cock and Nicola's dildo. Then Nicola began to scream as Sara furiously fucked Nicola's ass and fingered her pussy, I pulled my cock out of Sara's ass and Nicola grabbed it and began to bite and suck it bringing me back to the verge of cumming.

I moved away from both women and led on my back and put a pillow under my ass to raise my cock up.

"Right Nicola I want you put my cock inside your ass and Sara I want you rubbing your hot cunt in my face". Nicola leant across me her heavy breasts felt hot against my skin, slowly she lowered herself onto my cock. Nicola's ass hole well lubricated and stretched by Sara, but it still took a little wiggle of her hips to let me slide inside. As Nicola sat up I could feel my cock being gripped as her anus tightened around it. Sara stood over me with her back to Nicola, she stood there stroking her pussy and spreading her lips with her fingers,

Nicola picked up a dildo and pushed inside Sara's pussy, Sara's backed arched as the dildo slipped in she rubbed her clit hard, Nicola picked up the second toy and firmly rammed it into Sara's ass, Sara gasped with pleasure, with this fantastic view I grabbed Nicola's thighs I rocked her ass hole up and down my cock.

Sara said she was about to cum and Nicola took the toys

from her and Sara lowered her dripping pulsating cunt onto my mouth her juices tasted fantastic as they flowed from her pussy.

Nicola's was fingering her own pussy at the same time and her anus began to squeeze my cock almost painfully as she had another orgasm, I couldn't hold on any longer and shot my cum inside her ass. We all collapsed on the bed, Sara and I stroking Nicola's breasts and pussy, while we all gathered our breath, Sara smiling at me I knew she had enjoyed herself and I had satisfied my customer.

BI- MALES
Forced Bi Story

My sessions with Peter were had grown more intense. He had been the subject of an anal gang bang and been pissed on. He'd had clothespins flogged from his ball sac. He had even requested to be waterboarded, but I didn't know how to do that safely. There was one more taboo, though, and I wanted him to try it.

I wanted to see him get fucked by a guy.

We had talked extensively about our sex lives, and I knew he'd never tried this. He wasn't hung up about gay sex — I'd seen him greet gay friends with a kiss on the cheek — it just didn't turn him on. I even though about asking him if I could a guy fuck him, but I didn't. I thought he'd say yes. And I thought he'd have a better time if I could introduce an element of non-consent. And it would be hotter for me as well.

That said, what I was going to do was more than a bit cruel. So I decided I would make it up to him with something I knew he wanted very much — my pussy. For the first time since college, I'd fuck a guy.

And that is how I found myself once again at Rebecca's Hidden Chamber with Peter. I had blindfolded him and cuffed his wrists to the suspension bar handing from the ceiling. My strap-on was deep in his ass, and he was enjoying the last wisps of an anal orgasm. I pulled out and let him hang there — he was too far gone to stand up.

I got my phone and sent a short text. Half a minute later, there was a knock at the door.

"Are you ready for your surprise?" I asked Peter.

The last time I had a surprise for him was the anal gang bang, so I knew he'd be psyched.

"Yes, please, Mistress Kathi."

I opened door, and Rico and Michael walked in. They were friends of mine, and had been dating for a while. When I approached them with the idea of fucking a straight dude, they nearly jumped out of their skins with excitement. I had arranged for them to come to the dungeon and hang out in a spare room.

 I toldthem when to be ready, and that they'd better be hard and wrapped.

Michael walked up behind Peter quietly.

"Are you ready for some ass-fucking, Peter?" I asked.

"Fuck yeah," he said. "You know I love it. Fuck my ass!"

Michael spread some lube on his cock, and spread Peter's cheeks. I snuck around for a better view. I saw Michael push the head of his cock into Peter's anus, and I saw Peter slide his ass down the shaft.

He moaned with satisfaction.

Michael found his rhythm, and started pounding Peter's ass in earnest. Peter was loving it, oblivious to the fact he had a real cock inside him. His face was contorted in pleasure, moaning loudly. I watched him quiver his way through another anal orgasm.

I motioned for Michael to move and Rico took his place.

"Ready for cock #2?" I asked. "Give me that cock!" he said.

Little did he know.

Rico slid into Peter's ass and started fucking him.

I brought Michael in front of Peter and he removed his condom. Then I adjusted the suspension bar to lower Peter's face down towards Michael's cock.

"You ready for a cock in your mouth?"

"Yes, yes, yes," he moaned. "Give me cock!"

He opened his mouth, waiting for a cock to enter it. And then I removed the blindfold.

His face registered shock, seeing Michael standing nude and hard in front of him. Then he looked over his shoulder to find Rico plugging away at him. He dropped his head in shock and shame, then raised it to look at me.

He was confused. He was having his first gay experience, and he was enjoying it. At least the ass- fucking.

"Didn't I tell you how much I like gay porn?" I said. "Watching two guys go at it together. I think it's so hot."

"Sometimes I'd fantasize that you were one of the guys I was watching," I continued. "And I would jerk off so hard. I wanted to see it — I wanted to see you get fucked by a man." I walked over to Peter and stroked his head.

"Now I'd like to watch you suck cock. Will you do that for me?"

He looked up at me, and then slowly opened his mouth. He didn't want to do this, but he'd do it for me.

Michael stepped forward and placed his cock in Peter's mouth. Peter closed his eyes and started sucking.

"Open your eyes, Peter. Look at the man who's going to face-fuck you."

He obeyed, and Michael pushed further into Peter's mouth. I heard Peter gag, then saw him drop his jaw to allow entry to his throat.

Peter was getting fucked up the ass and deep-throating at the same time. This was awesome.

I took off my strap-on and got a vibrator. I got on the bed and started masturbating, taking in my own personal sex show. Peter looked over at me, and I think he realized he was the center of attention (again). He started sucking and fucking harder.

"Peter, look at me now," I said. "Know I'm cumming to the

sight of you being fucked by men."

I mashed the Hitachi into my clit, and an orgasm exploded in my brain.

"OK, guys, hold on. Let's move onto to Peter's treat."

The guys pulled out, and I uncuffed Peter. He straightened up and I kissed him. It was weird to taste another man's cock on his lips. I maneuvered him onto the bed. I put his ass near the edge, so Michael could fuck him some more. Rico took off his rubber and positioned himself by Peter's head. I climbed on top of Peter, straddling him with my knees.

"Peter, I know you want to fuck me, and I'm going to let you. But I want your forced bi experience to continue. Is that OK?"

"Oh, God, yes."

Michael put his cock back in Peter's ass, and Rico slapped Peter's face with his cock. I grabbed Peter's cock, rubbed it against my pussy, then slid it into me. It was like he was getting DP-ed.

Peter opened his mouth and sucked Rico's cock. I laid down on top of Peter and licked at Rico's cock. Then Peter and I took turns, Rico's cock sliding in and out of our mouths. I bounced up and down on Peter's cock, enjoying the sensation of a live cock in my pussy.

I fucked Peter harder. And I felt his hips come up meet mine, stroke for stroke. I knew he'd wanted to fuck me since we met, but he thought he'd never have a chance. So it was a little like a dream come true for him. All he had to do was get fucked by men.

And eat some cum.

Rico was grunting. He pulled out of Peter's mouth and started jerking his cock. Peter opened his mouth, because he knew what he was here for. Rico exploded in his mouth, with a couple of drops of his semen landing on Peter's cheek. I sucked them up and spat them into Peter's mouth.

"Don't swallow," I said, "don't dare fucking swallow."

He kept the cum in his mouth as I continued to fuck him. I felt Michael's hands on my hips as he plowed into Peter's ass. Peter's eyes closed and I felt his hips buck. Another anal orgasm.

Michael pulled out. He was ready to cum, too. He ripped off his condom and placed himself by Peter's head. Peter opened his mouth, and I saw Rico's cum again. Michael jerked his cock, and Peter's mouth filled with even more cum.

I put my hands on Peter's chest to get leverage on his dick. I squeezed it as hard as I could, feeling it fill my pussy. I looked down and saw all that cum in Peter's mouth.

I came.

But Peter was still going. I squeezed his cock some more.

"Cum for me, Peter," I said, " and when you cum, cum inside me."

A few more strokes, and Peter's hips lifted me off the bed. He'd cum.

Quickly, I scampered up and put my pussy above Peter's mouth. I spread my pussy lips, and pushed his cum down into his mouth.

"Three loads, Peter. That's how much cum you've had today," I said. "And you look so fucking hot with that cum sitting in your mouth. Now swallow it for me."

And the cum was gone.

***

Rico and Michael headed off to the bathroom. I was alone with Peter.

"How was it?" I asked.

"Good," he said. "Weird. Different."

"Would you do it again?"

"I'd do it for you," he said. "That was the hottest part — knowing you were watching me get fucked. And getting turned on. I wanted to give you a good show."

"What was it like to have a real cock up your ass?" I asked.

"Pretty much the same. Maybe not quite as hard. But I was already high from on orgasm, so I wasn't really focusing on it. But the guys had good rhythm —"

"Michael and Rico. They're friends of mine."

"They're good."

"As good as me?"

"Nobody's as good as you," he said.

I smiled.

"What about sucking cock?" I asked.

"Definitely different. Different feel, different taste."

"You really do look good with a cock in your mouth." "The same could be said about you," he said.

I'd blown Peter a couple of times. That kind of behavior was forbidden at the Hidden Chamber, but sometimes a girl gets carried away. Or a guy.

"So ... are you gay now? Or bi?" I asked.

"What are you? Ready to go from dyke to bi?" "You've only

fucked me once, buster."

"Yeah, but it's going to happen again. 'Cause you liked it."

"We'll see," I said. "But yes, I liked fucking you. And you made me orgasm. So thank you."

"Thank you, Mistress Kathi."

***

Sadly, this will be the last I write of my times at Rebecca's Hidden Chamber. The next day, the dungeon was raided by the New York City police, and several of my friends were arrested on prostitution charges. The problem, it turned out, was that fucking a guy up the ass with a strap-on was considered prostitution, something I'd never heard of before.

The real reason, though, was real estate. Rebecca's was in what used to be a thoroughly unattractive portion of Manhattan (5th and 30th). But the real estate boom had changed the neighborhood, and we had started getting complaints from the new arrivals. It was only a matter of time before the moneyed interests shut down something that, while unsavory to some, provided a lot of pleasure to many.

My days as a pro-domme were dwindling. I would see Peter again, many times, and two or three other clients as well. Times change, and maybe I was, too. But I don't regret a thing about my time at Rebecca's. I had some great sex, made some good friends and got paid well. And I made a lot of men, and the odd woman or two, cum.

THE CATALYST
Forced Gangbang Story

It's not that our sex life had become irretrievably dull, no not at all. Ok, Pete was no stud but at least he always tried to make sure that I came, often before him. We tried out a variety of positions, some of which were more pleasurable to me, many of which really excited Pete, my partner for 20 years, and some which turned us both on and nearly always caused me to have multiple orgasms. So I really had nothing to complain about. It was just that … well, it seemed that sex was becoming routine and lacked the spark that once used to fire us with real passion. That's why we booked ourselves on an all-inclusive holiday in a 5-star hotel on the Mayan Riviera in Mexico in an effort to revitalize our sex life. The sensuality of the sun, sea and sand might just perk up life in the bedroom, we thought - that and being away from work and the staid, old home environment.

The catalyst for the wildest sexual experience I have ever encountered occurred on the second afternoon of our stay as Pete and I relaxed on sun loungers down by the pool. I was enjoying the sensuality of the sun and it almost as if it was caressing my body. I started to apply some suntan lotion, stroking it slowly over my legs, arms and stomach. I was then suddenly aware that I was being watched and, glancing over to the swim-up bar, noticed three young men, staring at me, and I was clearly the subject of their conversation. They were probably in their late twenties, but who cares when they were as good-looking as they were and had such well-formed, tanned bodies. Shame that their Speedos spoiled the view - but I have a vivid imagination and I pictured their cocks starting to get erect as they discussed what they'd like to do to me.

Pete had also noticed the three guys eyeing me up. "Hey, there are three guys over at the bar undressing you with their eyes. I think they fancy you."

"Don't be stupid," I said, "I must be twenty years older than them. There's any number of younger, sexier women around here. What would they want with a body like mine?"

"Are you kidding? You look great for your age – flat stomach, long slender legs, great tits. Besides, I know when a guy's attracted to someone. Look at them.

 If their tongues hang out any further they'll be licking the floor. Tell you what - tease them a bit. Go on!"

I squirted some more lotion over my stomach, making it look like a jet of spunk hitting me. I then proceeded to stroke it all over, slowly and provocatively, sliding my fingers enticingly and ever deeper into my bikini bottom until it must have looked as though I was massaging my clit. Not being able to resist the temptation, I glanced over to the swim-up bar and made eye contact with the three guys. They knew I was performing this mock-masturbation for their benefit and, judging by the steadily increasingly bulge in their Speedos; it was clearly having an effect.

I'd got myself worked up by now and suggested to Pete that we go back to our room. I pulled him through the door, threw my bag into a corner and slid my hand into his trunks. Firmly taking his cock in my hand I eased it out and began to stroke the shaft, feeling it grow hard.

"Strip me", I urged him.

Now naked, I knelt down in front of him, sliding off his trunks in the process. I then took his cock in my mouth, gently and teasingly at first, running the tip of my tongue around the head and then delicately pressing my teeth into the hardening shaft. I grasped his buttocks and slowly pulled him towards me taking the whole of his cock in my mouth and sucking him hard, as if to drink all the juices that were now beginning to flow.

"Fucking hell, Rose, that's great!" he gasped trying to catch his breath and pulling my head forward, pushing even more of his prick into my mouth and throat. "Where did you suddenly learn to do that?"

I hadn't the heart to tell him that I was still picturing the three guys down at the pool, this time completely naked and wanking while they watched me stroking my clit and occasionally pushing a finger into my cunt. Besides, I never speak with my mouth full.

Pete then picked me up, carried me over to the bed, and threw me on my back forcing my legs wide open and lifting them up in the air.

Then, thrusting his cock deep inside me, he began to pound away with all the lust and energy of a younger man who hadn't had a woman for years. We both came at the same time and I felt his spunk pumping inside me as I gripped his cock inside my vagina, drawing him in even further. We collapsed exhausted onto the bed and waited for the dizziness to subside.

"Wow, it's a long time since I've had an orgasm like that! You seemed to enjoy it as well. I wonder what brought that performance out of you," mused Pete, "though I think I've a pretty good idea what turned you on."

Nothing more needed to be said and anyhow I didn't feel like declaring my fantasy. I think he already had a pretty good idea.

The following afternoon we headed for the pool. I suggested trying to grab a couple of sun loungers near the swim-up bar. Pete's wry smile betrayed that he knew why I wanted to be at that particular spot. I had my fingers crossed that the three guys would be there again. I wasn't to be disappointed. When they looked over at me I smiled in return and immediately regretted it. It was as good as an admission that the performance of masturbation I'd given the day before was entirely for their benefit. Well ok, I know it was for their benefit but I kicked myself for effectively confessing it. The three guys smiled back knowingly.

"I'll go and get us a couple of drinks," said Pete a short while later. He headed over and stood directly next to the three guys, though there was plenty of space at the bar. I could see him in conversation with them and all four occasionally threw a smiling glance in my direction. When Pete returned with our cocktails (mine was a Mississippi mud, his a daiquiri) I was intrigued to discover what they'd been talking about.

"Oh nothing. Just chitchat. They're all from South Carolina

and this is their last day here. Chris is the blond guy, Andy's the tall one with the blue trunks and Phil's the guy that obviously works out at the gym a lot. Nice guys."

"Is that all you talked about?"

"Yes, that just about sums it up". That abruptly ended the conversation. We returned to our drinks.

Two or three cocktails later I was beginning to feel horny again, so suggested we go back to our room. Pete took no persuading. As we left I could see Chris, Andy and Phil finishing their drinks. I thought nothing more of it.

No sooner had we entered our room and I was in the process of loosening my hair than the door burst open and the three guys rushed in. Then there was one hell of a commotion. The door was slammed shut and locked. Pete was overpowered by the three guys and stripped of his trunks. He was then tied in an armchair facing the bed. They then turned towards me.

"It's our last day here," said Chris, "and we're going to make it a memorable one – for all of us. Any screaming by the way and we'll cut your husband." Andy brandished a long knife menacingly.

I was still in shock and couldn't have uttered a squeak even if I'd tried. All three guys then stripped in front of me and my eyes fixed on three huge cocks. Now, Pete's not lacking in that department but this was something else. I was dumbstruck.

"Do you like what you see, Rose? I hope so. Cos you're gonna get very familiar with these bad boys," said Phil. I was slowly coming to my senses and on hearing him use my name I realised that Pete must have been talking about me with them at the bar.

"Hey, we're all naked," said Chris slyly, "and Rose is still wearing her bikini. I think we oughta do something about that, fellas".

Chris and Phil quickly grabbed my arms while Andy stepped forward and cut the straps of my bikini to with his knife and then ripped it off and tossed it on the floor.

"Your wife's got lovely tits," said Andy, turning to address Pete. He proceeded to stroke and fondle them and bent forward to lick each nipple in turn.

Lightly pulling them with his teeth he then sucked each nipple until they were both hard and erect. Running his fingers down my stomach he slid them inside my bikini bottom and pulled so that he could insert his knife to cut the side straps and let it fall to the floor. I felt vulnerable and yet slightly aroused when I saw their eyes feasting on my naked body.

Andy knelt down in front of me and forced my legs apart. Turning to Pete he said, "Let's see if Rose smells and tastes as sweet as her name". I felt his cheeks against the inside of my thighs as he first sniffed my cunt then gently ran the tip of his tongue around the lips of my vagina and up and down the hood of my clit. I looked over at Pete expecting him to be struggling to free his bonds. To my horror his cock was stiff and hard and he was obviously so excited that his juices were running down the shaft. He's enjoying this, the swine, " I thought. Then the full realization hit home. Pete's no seven-stone weakling, yet it seemed to me that the guys had overpowered him pretty damn quickly and now he was getting turned on watching me about to be gangbanged by three total strangers. Well, two can play at that game or in this case four of us.

I pushed my hips forward to make Andy's job easier and let his agile tongue work its magic.

"That's it, baby", he said, "you enjoy it". His tongue now

stiffened and I felt the tip enter my cunt and lick inside me. I was beginning to get hot and wet.

"Our turn now, Rose. Kneel down", said Chris.

I immediately did as I was instructed and the three guys stood in front of me, their huge pricks beginning to get really hard now.

"Let's see if we can really get some life into these cocks of yours" I said. I was warming to the task and glanced over to Pete. If he thought he was going to watch me being raped then he had another think coming. I was going to enjoy this and make sure that he could see what pleasure it was giving me.

There was nothing he could do about it. I took as much of Andy's cock in my mouth as I could and moved my head forwards and backwards sucking hard all the time and giving Andy the most enormous erection. I let him fuck my mouth. I bet he'd never been as hard as that.

"Your wife gives a good blowjob," said Andy catching his breath, "I hope I don't come too soon"

While I was giving Andy good head I slowly massaged

Chris's and Phil's cocks lubricating them with their own juices. Their powerful cocks in my hands and Andy desperately trying not to climax gave me a feeling of great power and I too became tremendously excited, to the extent that I wanted to behave like a sex-starved whore.

"Fuck me," I said to them, "any way you'd like".

The three guys needed no further invitation. I was lifted onto the bed and Chris was the first in taking me from behind doggy-style. Phil knelt in front and pushed his bulging cock into my mouth.

"I love watching a spit roast", said Andy who was wanking while enjoying the spectacle.

"Your wife's cunt is hot – and wet!" said Chris, "Do want to know how wet, Pete?"

Chris then withdrew, walked over to Pete and thrust his cock, glistening with my juices, into Pete's mouth.

"Suck on that!" he said, as he fucked Pete's mouth.

This got me unbearably excited. I pulled away from Phi's cock and demanded that all three guys fuck me at the same time.

Phil lay on his back on the bed. "Bring Rose over here. I want to fuck that sweet arse. Andy and Chris picked me up, spread my legs and slowly lowered me so that Phil could enter my bottom. His cock was well lubricated and the head slipped in quite easily.

"She's got a lovely tight arse your wife, Pete. Haven't you given her anal sex before? Let's go a bit deeper."

It hurt at first then the pain subsided as his stiff cock penetrated deeper and deeper into my bottom and I looked hungrily at Andy. He knelt between my spread- eagled legs insert the head of his cock into my now dripping cunt and pushed all the way in until his groin was massaging my clit. Phil and Andy synchronized their thrusting and pumped their huge pricks rhythmically in and out of me.

"Let me fill that remaining hole," said Chris, straddling my face and pushing his cock into my mouth. I sucked him hard at the same time wrapping my tongue around the head of his prick.

All three guys were pounding away now, grunting and

moaning in ecstasy and seeming to sink their cocks ever deeper inside me. I could hear Pete moaning, clearly frustrated that he couldn't touch his cock, which was now covered in his juices.

The three guys were now nearing their climax. I grabbed Andy's buttocks, sinking my nails into his firm arse and pulled him tightly towards me. I wanted the whole of his cock inside me when he came.

Chris was the first to reach an orgasm and I felt him spend his load deep in my bottom. This caused Andy to come almost at the same time, as he must have been able to feel Chris's throbbing cock against his. He shot his hot spunk inside me. This was too much for me, and my climax, which had been inexorably building, burst with a dizzying display of fireworks and a tidal wave of pleasure as Chris filled my mouth with spunk. I was loath to swallow so let it spill out of the sides of my mouth, down my chin and onto my breasts.

This scene was too much for Pete. He let out a cry of relief after excruciating, pent-up frustration and shot a stream of spunk that reached his chin and covered his chest and stomach.

It seemed like hours until we all regained our composure but was probably only minutes. The guys donned their swimming trunks and made to leave.

"Hey, guys!" I said, "Safe journey home. And thanks."

"You're welcome. Any time!" they chorused and closed the door softly behind them.

I set Pete free. We embraced each and cuddled on the bed.

"This is going to be a great holiday, Pete" "You know, Rose. I think you're right."

We both looked forward to further adventures yet to come on this holiday.

www.ingramcontent.com/pod-product-compliance
Lightning Source LLC
Chambersburg PA
CBHW071248150726
48001CB00018B/463